LIVE BAIT

LIVE BAIT

BILL KNOX

Constable • London

Constable & Robinson Ltd
3 The Lanchesters
162 Fulham Palace Road
London W6 9ER
www.constablerobinson.com

First published in Great Britain 1978
This edition published in Great Britain by Constable,
an imprint of Constable & Robinson Ltd 2010

A copy of the British Library Cataloguing in Publication
Data is available from the British Library.

UK ISBN: 978-1-84901-347-5

Printed and bound in the EU

PEFC

PEFC/16-33-111
CATG-PEFC-052
www.pefc.org

Prelude

The man with the dark blue business suit and the mild brown eyes sat alone at a corner table in the otherwise busy hotel bar, troubling no one and hardly noticed. He was drinking malt whisky with water, each sip well spaced and savoured. He had been in the bar an hour and was on his fourth glass, each a different brand of malt ordered after a careful consideration of the gantry display.

Now and again he glanced casually at the customers at the other tables. They hardly interested him beyond the fact that several wore airline uniforms and that made him think of the airport a few minutes' drive away.

Tomorrow he would be home. His money would be waiting, to be paid on delivery. What happened after that was for someone else to decide.

The man took another sip of the drink in front of him. It was an Auchentoshan, one of the many single malt whiskies he had discovered during the last few days. They seemed part of the Scottish cultural experience and if he was told to make another trip to Scotland he –

The door of the bar was flung open and uniformed figures came surging in. The man tensed instinctively,

1

then just as quickly relaxed again. The new arrivals were more airline staff, three Swissair crewmen and a couple of hostesses, and they went straight across to join a K.L.M. group at one of the tables.

One of the girls was a tall, slim redhead. Their eyes met as she leaned forward to accept a cigarette and a light from one of the K.L.M. people, but the fact didn't seem to register with her.

The man sighed a little to himself. Being the type of person who was ignored was part of his stock in trade, like his soberly cut business suit and middle-aged haircut. He watched the redhead a moment longer, wondering if she'd ever really considered the health hazards that went with smoking. It was a habit he'd long since given up.

Finishing his drink, he glanced at his wristwatch. It was getting late, he would have to be up early to catch his flight in the morning, and he always made it a rule to take a short walk before retiring. It toned up the system, ensured sound sleep.

He rose, nodded a polite goodnight to the barman, and went out. Once in the hotel lobby, he hesitated and thought about going up to his room to get his overcoat. Then, shrugging, he went out through the main doors and exchanged the brightly lit warmth for the chill of the night air.

Breath clouding like mist, he began walking. The whisky, he noted, seemed to be generating its own warmth and well-being and as he reached the end of the hotel driveway he turned right, on to the main road. When he'd arrived, he'd noticed a bridge over a river not far along. There and back should be just about right.

Swinging his arms, humming under his breath, he began striding along the verge. An occasional car went past, bathing him in light for a moment, then as he rounded a bend he saw the silhouette of the bridge ahead in the faint moonlight, the glint of the river, and what looked like the lights of a small boat.

The boat interested him. Deciding he would get a better view from the other side of the road, he waited to let a truck go past, then started to cross.

He was halfway over when he heard the car come round the bend. It was travelling fast, too fast, and he glanced round quickly.

In the very few seconds that remained the man in the dark business suit just had time to realize that the car was weaving from side to side – and that it was going to hit him.

The last thing he saw, apart from the headlights, was two white blobs of faces staring at him from behind the windscreen. Then the car smashed into him. He was thrown into the air, a bundle of arms and legs that landed on the car roof before it was flung back on to the roadway.

Skidding wildly, shedding headlamp glass, the car mounted the grass verge, bounced savagely, then somehow emerged on the road again. For a moment it almost stopped rolling, then the engine bellowed and it accelerated away, becoming two red tail lights which disappeared round the next bend.

It was two minutes later before another car came along, caught the limp figure sprawled on the road in its headlamp beams, and stopped. The driver wore a dinner jacket, his wife was in a long dress, and they found that the man lying in the roadway in that spreading pool of blood was still just alive.

The driver hesitated, thinking of the amount he'd had to drink and how he'd stand up to a police breathalyser test. He told his wife to say she'd been behind the wheel, then saw another vehicle approaching and flagged it down. The new arrival was an airport service van, and it had a radio. The van driver radioed for police and an ambulance.

The man in the dark blue business suit died where he lay while the acknowledgement crackled back.

Three miles further on, a damaged car lurched to a halt on a patch of waste ground within sight of the lights of a town.

Two fifteen-year-old boys scrambled out and began running. They had stolen the car from a city parking lot after missing their last bus home.

It was twenty minutes later when they reached their own street. One had been physically sick along the way, they parted still too frightened to talk – and they spent the next few weeks in a state of terror every time they saw a police uniform.

But they were never caught.

Chapter One

It was Tuesday and a typically crisp Scottish autumn morning, the kind that left a dusting of white frost along roofs on the little street of identical little bungalows. But as he finished shaving and considered himself in the mirror, Detective Chief Inspector Colin Thane, head of Glasgow Millside Division C.I.D., Strathclyde Police, knew the uneasy chill he felt had nothing to do with the weather.

Colin Thane had joined the old City of Glasgow force as a beat cop and had come up fast, the hard way. A tall, grey-eyed man with dark, thick hair and a rugged, naturally cheerful face, he still had the muscular build which went back to when he'd been younger, a few pounds lighter, and a fair to reasonable amateur boxer. He'd learned a lot since then, like how to fight dirty in a backstreet brawl if you wanted to survive.

But this was different.

Some things were as usual. His wife, Mary, was already downstairs, getting breakfast for their two children. Tommy and Kate were creating their usual racket, trying to find schoolbooks and eat at the same time.

But Thane's best suit, a lightweight grey wool, had

5

been laid out for him along with a clean shirt and Mary's choice of tie and handkerchief. He didn't like the tie but he wasn't going to argue about it, not today.

It was Promotions Day. Thane smiled wryly as he dressed, knotted the tie, pulled on his jacket, and filled his pockets.

When he left home, he was to go straight to Headquarters. When he emerged from there, he'd be Detective Superintendent Thane, and reaching superintendent rank at the age of forty-two rated as quite an achievement in any police force. It also meant more money, which he certainly could use.

Except he wouldn't be going back to Millside Division. All he'd been told so far was that he would be 'reassigned', and no amount of tapping the normally reliable grapevine had been able to glean more. Which left his future wide open, from a Headquarters desk job to the equally unhappy prospect of a posting to some distant backwoods.

In a couple of hours he'd know the worst. Thane looked at the tie again, cursed the relative who had given him it as a birthday present, and headed downstairs. Clyde, the family's brindle Boxer dog, was sprawled out on the half-landing and Thane had to step over him. The dog looked up briefly, gave a half-hearted twitch of a tail-stump, then went back to sleep.

Breakfast amounted to the two children across the table from him having a small war about something while he ate. Then they left for school, Mary collapsed into a chair beside him, and they had time for another cup of coffee and a cigarette before a car horn sounded outside.

She came to the door to see him off, a slim, attractive, dark-haired woman who still wore the same dress size as when they'd married. Mostly, she claimed, they were still the same dresses.

'Good luck.' A twinkle in her eyes, she straightened his tie and kissed him. 'Try and look happier when you get there – and give Phil my love when you see him.'

He nodded absently. Detective Inspector Phil Moss, his number two all the time he'd been at Millside, was in hospital recovering from surgery. When he was fit for duty again Moss was also going to be reassigned and didn't know where. It was all change time.

Leaving Mary, he crossed their tiny strip of front garden, then stopped at the kerb and raised a surprised eyebrow. The waiting divisional C.I.D. car was washed and polished like he'd never seen it before. The driver not only stood ready to open the front passenger door, which was more than unusual, but saluted him for the first time in years.

Then, when they set off, the route was different too – a curve through the heart of Millside Division, anything but a short cut towards the city centre and Headquarters. Somehow, just about every road junction seemed to have a Division car idling around so that it could flash its lights or give a horn-blast and from the grin on his driver's face it had all been very obviously and carefully arranged.

Touched more than he wanted to show, Thane settled back in his seat as they left Millside territory and the high-rise office blocks and shopping streets of the city centre began.

He'd miss Millside Division. It was a sprawling, ugly slice of Glasgow dockland on the River Clyde, backed by everything from slums and factories to a high-amenity fringe. It had a crime rate which made most social planners wish it could be towed out to sea and sunk – yet it had been his parish, one he'd come to know and understand in a perverse liking.

So what were Headquarters playing at, what were they planning to do with him?

He still wasn't any nearer guessing an answer when, minutes later, the duty car pulled in outside the main door at Headquarters. Thane got out and the car drove off again like a symbol on its own.

Turning, taking a deep breath, Thane glanced up at the tall brick-faced building which was the nerve-centre for the largest police force in Britain after London's Metropolitan mob, then went in through the glass doors.

The Headquarters lobby had a squad of young police cadets on duty as ushers, wearing white gloves for the occasion. One lanky, pimple-faced teenager guided Thane into the nearest lift like a package for delivery. When they got out again, they went through a set of swing doors and reached the Promised Land – the private, carpeted corridor which led to the chief constable's office.

The cadet left him there, at the end of a small queue of other officers, men and women, similarly summoned to go through the promotion machine. Some were in uniform, others in plain clothes, and a few whose faces he knew gave a wink or a sheepish grin. Before he'd got used to his surroundings, two more candidates had arrived and were waiting behind him.

The queue moved steadily, being processed through a door ahead at the rate of one every couple of minutes. A young, blonde policewoman ahead of him was being made up to sergeant and looked tense enough to burst into tears. Ahead of her an elderly, florid-faced chief inspector with a double row of medal ribbons on his tunic shuffled his feet and kept glancing at his watch.

One after another they went through the door and emerged again. Then, at last, it was Thane's turn. An orderly led him through into the spacious, plainly furnished office. The thin, soft-spoken man behind the large desk got up, gave him a handshake, spoke a few words of formal congratulation, then paused. A pair of cool, unemotional eyes considered Thane thoughtfully for a moment.

'I know your record, Detective Superintendent.' It was the first time Thane had been addressed that way, and it sounded odd. 'It tells me all I think I need to know. For instance, I understand the administrative paperwork coming out of Millside Division can only improve.'

'Yes, sir.' Thane kept his face expressionless.

'It takes all kinds.' He gave a fractional smile. 'Thank heaven, we've got them. Now, there should be someone outside waiting to see you.'

The interview was over. Thane left, brushing shoulders with a detective sergeant being ferried in, and a moment later, back in the corridor, a heavy hand fell on his shoulder.

'Well, you made it,' boomed a cheerful voice. William 'Buddha' Ilford, the large, heavy-jowled man in a hairy tweed suit who stood at his elbow, was an assistant chief constable, which put him up among the archangels. But he didn't believe in formality. Standing back a pace, he inspected Thane carefully. 'Now, what the hell can we do with one brand new detective superintendent? How about a nice, quiet school patrol duty somewhere?'

'Have you seen the average school lately? I couldn't last the pace, sir.' Thane knew Ilford was the man who could decide, despite the joviality. An unpredictable bear of a man with thinning grey hair, he had been the city's C.I.D. boss for many years. Now, as an assistant chief constable, he fulfilled the same role in the larger amalgam of territories which made up the Strathclyde Region force. 'Still, I might take it – I've been feeling like I was in cold storage.'

'You're right.' Ilford gave a slight frown. 'But we haven't been playing games. That's why I'm here.'

He beckoned, and led Thane along the Promised Land corridor to his own office, opened the door, and waved Thane in. It was an untidy room, the desk littered with papers, the walls cluttered with old, framed photographs which spanned a career. There was a man standing in the middle of it all, studying one of the photographs. He was quietly dressed, medium height and build, and had iron-grey hair. He turned to face them as Ilford closed the door.

'You found him then.' The grey-haired man, who looked mild enough to be someone's benevolent bank manager, took a limping step forward. 'Congratulations, Superintendent. You maybe don't remember me.'

But Thane did, because of the limp. His name was Tom Maxwell and they'd worked together three years before when an armed robbery team wanted in Glasgow had been flushed out of its farmhouse hide-out. Maxwell had been a county cop, a police marksman, and that was the day he'd acquired his limp – falling off a roof while chasing one of the gang who had just come near to killing another cop with an axe.

'Detective Superintendent Maxwell,' said Ilford almost conversationally. 'He's deputy commander of the Scottish Crime Squad. You'll be working with him – under him.' He grinned at Maxwell as he spoke. 'That's for the record, Tom; from now on he's your problem.'

Thane stared at Ilford first, then at Maxwell, startled.

'Sorry you couldn't be told earlier,' said Maxwell mildly. 'We've been having budget problems. Most of our money comes from Central Government and it looked like we'd have to choose between you and a new coffee pot. But the commander wanted you and put a squeeze on.' He shrugged. 'We got approval yesterday.'

'I'm glad,' said Thane weakly.

He'd landed lucky, luckier than he could have hoped. The Scottish Crime Squad was a small, hand-picked unit which worked independently, free of ties to any regional force. It could prowl the country at will, mostly choosing its own targets – and any criminal operation which became an S.C.S. target was major. An S.C.S. posting was the kind of chance most working cops dreamed about.

'Yes, that application you made couldn't have been better timed,' said Buddha Ilford slyly. He turned away, opening a cupboard and bringing out a bottle and glasses. 'It calls for a drink.'

'Sir?' Thane blinked, wondering what Ilford meant. But the assistant chief constable was busy, pouring a stiff measure of whisky into each of three glasses, then adding a mist of water from a jug.

'Nice to see it work out,' said Superintendent Maxwell happily. 'We're choosy, but we can only select from volunteers. It's – ah – the usual deal, of course. You're on attachment from your own force, like the rest of us.'

'Till they throw you out or we want you back.' Ilford ambled over and handed them their drinks. He took a gulp from his own. 'Here's to crime.'

'Keeps us in a job.' Thane completed the toast and took a cautious sip. He knew he'd been caught up in some kind of conspiracy. 'When do I start?'

'Tomorrow.' Maxwell glanced at Buddha Ilford, drew a faint nod of approval, and went on briskly. 'We're putting you straight to work – we've got hold of something which can't wait.'

'Better tell him,' said Ilford dryly.

'Sir.' Maxwell leaned against the desk, nursing his drink, but now totally businesslike. 'Two nights back a Dane named Carl Pender was killed in a hit-and-run accident near Glasgow Airport. It was a stolen car, dumped afterwards.'

'Kids,' said Ilford. 'A couple of teenagers were seen prowling near the parking lot where the car was stolen. They jump-wired the ignition, one of the benefits of modern education.' He gave a shrug. 'We've no chance of getting them, but the local traffic cops are satisfied it was an accident.'

'So the interest is Pender?' asked Thane.

'Right,' agreed Maxwell. 'He'd been in Scotland a week, made noises about just having finished a touring holiday, and he was booked to fly back to Copenhagen the next morning.' He paused long enough to take a sip from his glass. 'All we really know about that week is that he had a Firth Agency self-drive car, rented from their airport branch – he'd

12

returned it that afternoon, just before he booked in for the night at the Shennan Hotel.'

'Just a plain, ordinary tourist?' Thane raised an eyebrow in open disbelief.

'That's how it looked,' admitted Maxwell. 'At least till one of the local cops, a fairly bright sergeant, collected Pender's belongings from his hotel room the next morning. You see, he found two small sachets of white powder hidden inside a spare pair of socks and had sense enough to decide he'd better have the powder analysed.'

Ilford nodded and stole the other man's punch line. 'Just as well – the preliminary lab report says it is a high-grade amphetamine. Lift-off stuff for any junkie, worth ten pounds a gram minimum.'

Thane waited, knowing there had to be more. But so far it sounded like a routine case for the Drug Squad team, nothing that rated a high priority.

'So we did a bit more checking on Pender,' said Maxwell grimly, as if reading his mind. 'His passport said he was a bookseller. The Danish police say they knew him as a suspected courier, a top-line errand boy in the European drugs scene. This time, they didn't even know he'd left home.'

'So somebody over there is getting his backside kicked.' Ilford's heavy jowls quivered a little. 'Hamlet strikes again.'

'Yes.' Maxwell forced an attempt at a smile which acknowledged that Ilford was an assistant chief constable, then kept on. 'Thane, if we're right, then Pender being killed has given us the break we've been waiting on, the reason why this is a Scottish Crime Squad target operation.' He finished his drink and set his glass down carefully. 'We reckon Pender got these two sachets of amphetamine over here, and that he had a very important reason for taking them back to his bosses – whether that means Copenhagen or deeper into Europe.'

Totally puzzled, Thane glanced at Ilford. But Ilford had lapsed into a deliberate silence, blandly contemplating his waistcoat in the habitual, annoying way which had won him his nickname. There was no immediate explanation coming from that direction.

'Do I get to hear why?' asked Thane with a degree of sarcasm.

'There's a file. It's yours from tomorrow.' Maxwell slipped back into his friendly bank manager pose, making it clear he wasn't going to be hurried. 'You've got to understand the way we work, Thane – sometimes it's a business of watching, waiting, then going in hard. Or we notice patterns, crimes in different regions that may have a common factor the local cops don't always spot.'

A heavy sniff came as a background noise from Ilford. It brought a slight smile from Maxwell, an indication the two men had already differed on that viewpoint. Then Maxwell went on in the same methodical way.

'About four months ago, in early summer, we noticed a minor rash of armed hold-ups, none of them big enough to matter on their own. The pattern was always roughly the same. A small team, hitting out-of-town post offices, places always far apart, and ignoring everything except cash.' Maxwell paused and shrugged. 'None of the local forces involved could come up with a really concrete lead. Then it all stopped, just as suddenly as it had begun.'

'I heard about them,' said Thane, the details a vague memory. 'They worked like pros, but –'

'But they didn't match up with any of the regular teams,' agreed Maxwell. 'To be honest, our people weren't particularly interested at the time. It wasn't a big enough operation, just six raids and the total haul around ten thousand pounds. We'd better fish to fry – or so we thought.'

'My turn,' said Buddha Ilford. 'Let me claim a little credit for Strathclyde. One of the post office raids was in Strathclyde territory. In it, a shot was fired into the ceiling to – ah – persuade the post office staff to co-operate. We retrieved the bullet, and identified it as from a nine mil. Luger pistol.'

Maxwell grinned. 'Which was our first piece of luck. The second came a couple of months ago, not long after the post office hold-ups ended. This time, it was a weekend break-in at a chemical supply warehouse in Edinburgh. Four men were involved, and they used a medium-sized van, colour blue, make unknown.'

'Someone saw them?' asked Thane.

'A watchman, who got a bullet in his leg for his trouble. Like to take a guess?'

'A nine mil. Luger?'

Maxwell nodded. 'Same gun. The team made a show of ransacking the warehouse office, then hauled off several drums of industrial chemicals.' He slapped a hand hard on Ilford's desk. 'I'll give them that they tried hard to make it look a haphazard selection, but it happened to include just about every raw material anyone would need to set up an amphetamine production plant. Now do you see the picture?'

15

Everything fitted. A skilfully planned operation which had begun with the small-scale armed hold-ups to raise funds, the warehouse break-in to collect raw materials, and finally Carl Pender. The Scottish Crime Squad interest was fully justified. It made clear sense that Pender had come to Scotland to collect samples of a first amphetamine production run, a preliminary to a major purchase by some European syndicate.

'How long till the laboratory tests are completed?' asked Thane.

'The forensic mob want another twenty-four hours, minimum, and that's pushing them hard.' Maxwell glanced at his wristwatch, then at Buddha Ilford. 'Thanks for arranging the meeting, sir. I reckon it's been helpful – all round.' He turned to Thane again, his smile back in place. 'See you tomorrow. You know the place, make it about 9 a.m. Okay?'

Thane nodded.

Limping across to the door, Maxwell went out. As the door closed again, Buddha Ilford settled in the leather chair behind his desk and began stuffing tobacco into the charred briar relic he called a pipe.

'Sit down and finish your drink,' he invited, a twinkle in his eyes. Then, as Thane obeyed, he asked almost innocently, 'So, how do you feel now?'

'Like I've been dropped in at the deep end.' Thane's eyes strayed to the photographs on the walls. A few went further back than Ilford's time – Victorian cops in heavy, old-style uniforms and strangely shaped helmets. Some carried swords. One magnificently bearded sergeant stood beside the barrow once used to wheel drunks in from the gutters to a cell. They'd had their own problems, but he wondered how they'd react to the way things were now. Drawing a breath, he eyed Ilford thoughtfully. 'You said I volunteered. When?'

'I forget.' Ilford struck a match and got the pipe going. Then, as it billowed to his satisfaction, he tossed the spent match into a massive ashtray. 'The chance came up, and I had a talk with the S.C.S. commander. But, of course, if you don't like the idea –'

Thane grinned. 'I could think of worse.'

'So could I,' said Ilford. 'If I hadn't sold them on the few better sides of your undiplomatic character you might have found that out. We've a surplus of chiefs – foot-slogging Indians are the ones in short supply.' He drew on his pipe again for a moment, his manner friendly but serious. 'It's a good chance, Colin. It'll give you the kind of experience that will matter when you come back to this force.'

Thane nodded, knowing Ilford wouldn't appreciate being thanked. Then, sensing the interview was over, he finished his drink and got to his feet.

'About this pay-off party tonight,' said Ilford unexpectedly. 'Tell your lads to charge a round of drinks to me. A pity you won't have Phil Moss along. How long is it now?'

'Four days since they operated,' said Thane. 'I'm visiting him this afternoon.'

'Moss without his stomach ulcer.' Ilford shook his head. 'It'll be a strange and new experience – may even civilize him. Right, tell him I'm saving up to bring some grapes.'

'I'll do that,' promised Thane. He crossed to the door, started to open it, then glanced back. 'I'll be doing my best.'

'You'd better,' said Ilford. 'I laid a ten pound side-bet with Tom Maxwell that you'd locate this

17

amphetamine mob and have them mopped up within two weeks – and that's the money you're drinking tonight.'

For Colin Thane, the next few hours were busy because he made them that way. But first he found a telephone in an empty side room and called home.

'I knew they couldn't trust you with a desk job,' said Mary over the line when she heard he was Scottish Crime Squad. 'It sounds good. Right for you.'

'It can be a travelling job,' he warned. 'No regular routine.'

'Since when did you have one?' she asked wryly. 'When they invented policemen they didn't exactly build in domestic bliss. But I know what I married.'

'Just as well.' He smiled at the phone, knowing she meant it. 'I'll tell you the rest of what happened when I get back tonight.'

'After your pay-off?' He heard her chuckle. 'No way. I'll be in bed. If I stay awake till then, it won't be so you can talk about work.'

He laughed, said goodbye, and hung up. Then, lighting a cigarette, he knew what he had to do next. Tomorrow he'd have the Scottish Crime Squad file and whatever it contained. But he'd still be the new boy in their firm – any advance homework he put in couldn't go wrong.

He started by talking to a grey-haired detective inspector who was duty officer in Criminal Intelligence, a quietly busy sector which was a world of filing cabinets, charts, and computer cards. After that, he moved back and forward between there and the Regional Drug Squad office, telling neither department anything specific but carefully gathering any crumbs they had available.

What he got on the drug scene didn't add up to much more than he'd known as a divisional officer. Scots still preferred their traditional vices of alcohol and gambling. Glasgow mainly rated as an underworld staging post for drugs coming into Britain, usually slab cannabis being smuggled in through her harbour docks or heroin packages trickling in at her airport.

'We're just a pause in the Far East trade to London and Europe, sir,' said one of the Drug Squad team. She was a young, good-looking redhead, a detective sergeant who could and sometimes did pass as being straight out of school. 'Of course, we've got our local quota of addicts and pushers, but we're low down the league table compared with most places in Europe.'

But the Drug Squad had no word of new pushers on the local scene, no upsurge in the amount of drugs being offered around, and certainly no hint of any new source of amphetamines having been felt on the market.

Criminal Intelligence eventually gave him a few files to read at a spare desk. He settled to the task hopefully – Criminal Intelligence thrived on other people's discards, on stray rumour and gossip, on such outward trivia as a known criminal being spotted with a new girlfriend. Weaving the strands, seeking for patterns, they usually could give some small hint or pointer.

But not this time. Thane smoked another couple of cigarettes and discarded his tight quota of nicotine for the day while he read through what he'd been given. There were details of the entire series of post office hold-ups and their out-of-town locations. In each case, a three-man team had taken part and had used a stolen getaway car. Two men, hooded and armed, always carried out the actual raid while the third man stayed with the car.

But after that any factual attempt at linking the raids was miserably weak. Witnesses gave descriptions which varied wildly when it came to the height, build and possible age of the hold-up trio.

It didn't surprise him. Allowing for human error, any experienced cop would have been startled if the witnesses had come up with identical details. Even the weapons used varied – a pistol had been used in three raids, but a sawn-off shotgun had featured in the others. So he might be dealing with three men, or the team might have more to draw on and ring the changes.

The final file left him equally gloomy. It was the one in which Criminal Intelligence listed the results of its own gathering and sifting.

Any gossip about the hold-ups to filter through from the underworld grapevine was puzzled and confused. Slightly angry, too, because the underworld were the last people to like a mystery they didn't understand. The regular heavy men, irritated at having to cope with additional police attention, guessed that some fresh team had come poaching into their territory – maybe a team which had sneaked up over the border from England, then had retired south again.

But it was always useful to blame the English. Proper, too – when they had similar problems, they blamed the Scots.

Thane returned the files and thanked the detective inspector. Then, surprised at how much time had

passed, he ate a quick, solitary lunch in the Headquarters canteen.

He finished, did without a cigarette, and cursed the
fact that he didn't have transport. It had been his own
idea that Mary have their rusted station wagon for the
day, which made sense when he thought of the pay-
off party ahead. But hospital visiting started in less
than half an hour and he didn't want to be late.

There was a drizzle of rain in the air when he left
Headquarters and walked to the bus stop at the next
corner. Then, for once, he was lucky. The bus he
wanted came along inside a couple of minutes and
though there was standing room only it trundled him
along to his destination, the Western Infirmary.

The rain was still coming down. He turned up his
coat collar, trudged to a kiosk to buy magazines and
a box of peppermint creams, then headed into the big,
ugly red sandstone hospital complex which was
Detective Inspector Phil Moss's temporary address.

Moss's surgical ward was on the second floor. He
reached it just as visiting time began and went in
through the doors on the tail of some other visitors.
As they spread out, Moss's thin, pale face grinned up
at him from one of the line of beds.

'How's the cut and weld job?' asked Thane, tossing
the magazines and peppermint creams on the bed.

'How the hell would I know? I'm just the patient,'
said Moss peevishly, reaching for the offerings.
'Typical medics – you're alive or you're dead and
they're not interested in between.'

'You're recovering,' agreed Thane.

He stood for a moment, a twinkle in his eyes, while
Moss examined the magazines. Small, mousy-haired,
in his late fifties, Detective Inspector Phil Moss was

a thin, wiry figure in rumpled pyjamas who looked indignantly out of place against the laundered white background of the hospital pillows and sheets.

But in some ways it was an improvement. Usually Moss looked on the verge of being a welfare case, with all the appearance of having slept in his clothes and being short of money for a shave and a haircut.

The rest was almost a legend in Millside Division. An abrasive, frequently acid-tongued bachelor with a methodical approach to life, Moss had fought off any suggestion of surgical cure for his duodenal ulcer for almost a decade. His do-it-yourself remedies and thunderous belches had been admired and talked about at least as much as his acknowledged ability as a hard-working cop.

Then, suddenly, he'd announced he was going in for a 'cut and weld' job – though the surgeon concerned preferred to call it a by-pass shunt operation.

For Phil Moss's sake, Thane had been glad. Despite their difference in years and just about everything else they had built up a friendship in their time together, and he had a notion that part of Moss's decision to accept surgery was linked with the fact that their working partnership at Millside Division was due to be broken up anyway.

'Mary said to say hello,' he said, bringing over a chair and sitting down at the bedside.

'Tell her the same.' Moss grinned for a moment then pointed at the peppermints. 'That's a lousy choice, but I'll swap it for something better.' He tossed the offending package aside, then settled back against the pillows with a grunt and a wince. 'Well, get to it. What job did they give you?'

'Scottish Crime Squad.'

'Not bad,' said Moss softly. He glanced round carefully. The bed on one side was empty, the patient nearest them was surrounded by a tribe of chattering family visitors. 'Handling what?'

'A backyard drug factory with a self-finance plan – or that's how it looks.' Thane told him the rest, keeping to basic details. Listening, Moss stopped being a hospital patient for the moment and became a cop again.

'A dead man makes a nice, easy start,' he said sardonically, then rubbed a thumbnail along the bedsheets. 'Why aren't you out talking to the people at his hotel?'

'I'm going,' said Thane dryly. 'Just as soon as I finish visiting the sick of this parish.'

'Do-gooder.' Moss elbowed himself up a fraction on the pillows and shook his head slightly. 'Well, good luck with it. I certainly won't be around to keep you out of trouble. Not unless you need an expert on bedpans or temperature charts.'

'My loss,' said Thane soberly. 'When are they going to open the cage and let you out?'

'In another ten days, they say – time off for good behaviour.' Moss was resigned. 'Then they reckon I'll need a month or so convalescent leave. After that – well, it'll be a medical downgrade and Buddha Ilford will hide me in a corner somewhere.'

'He's coming to see you.' Thane hesitated, knowing Moss could be right – and that if it happened, it would be a waste of his ability. 'You could be wrong.'

'Don't bet on it.' Moss looked across the ward and showed a sudden, only partly contrived interest. 'Well, well, the Vampire is on the prowl again.'

A tall, dark-haired nurse was talking to a patient in

23

a bed almost opposite, a heavily built man who lay staring at the ceiling and didn't seem to care what she was saying.

'Staff Nurse Blair,' said Moss acidly. 'She'd be a wow in the K.G.B. – probably trained there.'

Thane chuckled. 'Who's the patient?'

'John Gillan, an emergency appendix job. They brought him in last night and were operating almost before the ambulance stopped rolling.' Moss paused, seemed on the brink of adding something, then swore instead. The dark-haired nurse had turned away from the other bed and was heading in their direction.

'Your turn, Mr Moss,' she declared, reaching the bed. 'Feeling better?'

'I was,' said Moss pointedly.

'Good.' Her round, reasonably pleasant face shaped a tight smile. 'I want to take a look at your dressings. So, if your visitor doesn't mind –'

'I've got to go anyway,' said Thane, rising.

'At that, you're lucky,' muttered Moss. 'The motto here is Staff Nurse rules.'

'That's right.' The tight smile undented, she turned to Thane and one eyelid quivered in a suspicion of a wink. 'You know, our scrawny patients always heal quickly. Another couple of days and he'll have his stitches out.' She glanced back at Moss. 'That's something we can both look forward to, isn't it?'

Thane saw the light of battle in Moss's eyes, made quick goodbye noises, and beat a retreat as the screens were drawn around the bed.

The drizzle had ended and the streets were drying when he left the hospital. He boarded another bus

24

which took him to within a few hundred yards of Millside Police Station, then walked the remaining distance past the mixture of old tenement buildings and small shops which had become so familiar.

Millside Police Station was an old Victorian building, due for replacement but still in use because of budget cuts. It was an odd feeling going in, nodding as usual to the sergeant at the public counter, then trudging up the worn steps to C.I.D. territory. The main duty room was almost empty and Thane went through to his private office.

For a few days he'd been systematically clearing out his desk. Sorting through what was left, he tucked a few final items into a large envelope, then went out into the duty room again.

The man who was taking over from him was sitting quietly at a desk in the far corner. Dave Andrews was a tall, bald-headed chief inspector transferred from Headquarters, who had been around for a couple of weeks understudying the job but staying tactfully in the background.

'All yours now.' Thane laid his desk keys in front of Andrews, then placed the envelope beside them. 'Keep this for me, will you?'

'No problem,' Andrews assured him. 'The grapevine says you've done all right. Best of luck with it.'

'I'll need that.' For a moment Thane hesitated, feeling almost awkward. 'Dave, I'd like to borrow a car for a spell – if you've anything spare.'

'Need a driver?' asked Andrews.

Thane shook his head. 'Just wheels, for a couple of hours or so.'

'Then take mine.' Andrews leaned back and chuckled. 'Just make sure you're back in time for the pay-off party. It's the only damned thing that seems to matter around here today.'

The car was a two-year-old Volkswagen with a high polish, seat covers, and clean ashtrays. Andrews had no family and his wife worked in a law office. Driving the Volkswagen out of the police car park, heading for one of the entry points to the Clyde Tunnel, Thane thought of his own car again. Now that he had a detective superintendent's pay, he could probably afford to trade it in for something better.

It was a nice daydream, one that stayed with him as he travelled through the Clyde Tunnel, emerged on the south side of the river, and slotted into the motorway traffic heading west towards the airport. The traffic was busy but he made good time, then took a turn-off near the airport. A few minutes later he let the Volkswagen coast to a halt in the driveway outside the Shennan Hotel.

The Shennan was from the shoe-box school of architecture, a modern slice of glass and concrete construction. Inside, he crossed a carpeted lobby, showed his warrant card to the receptionist, and told him what he wanted.

'Sorry, I can't tell you anything about Mr Pender.' The receptionist, plump and tired-eyed, shook his head. 'I was on my day off, Superintendent. The only way I got involved was when I showed the police his room the next day.' He leaned forward, lowering his voice confidentially. 'But try Willie Cox, our barman. He says Pender was in the bar for a spell that night.'

The cocktail bar was across the lobby, to the right. Thane headed towards it, reached the entrance, then a figure stalking out almost collided with him. Thane heard a muttered apology, and a young man in a blue anorak went past, leaving him with a vague impression of a sallow face, long dark hair, and a glance which conveyed impatient indifference.

It was early and the bar held only a thin scatter of customers. Thane chose a quiet spot along the bar counter and repeated his performance with the warrant card when Willie Cox reached him.

'I want to talk about Carl Pender,' said Thane without preliminaries.

'He was here.' The barman, a small, sharp-faced man in shirt-sleeves, nodded cautiously. He had tattoo marks on both wrists and the general air of a man who didn't mind talking as long as he didn't get involved. 'He had a few drinks, on his own, and talked a little – that's all.'

'Did he tell you where he'd been while he was over here?' asked Thane.

'No.' Cox gave a slight smirk. 'Not the way you mean.'

'Then what?' Thane kept his patience.

'He talked about whisky – the malts.' The barman thumbed at the well-stocked gantry behind him. 'You know how it goes. Give a tourist a first taste of single malt whisky and it's as if they've found a new religion.'

Thane understood. To a native, Scotland's whisky was divided into two families. One family was made up of the commercial blends, the products of several malt distilleries bulked together with grain spirit. But the other family consisted of the more expensive pure malt whiskies. Each was the exclusive product of a single distillery, and each distillery's whisky had a character uniquely its own.

'Go on,' he encouraged softly. 'Where?'

27

'He knew Glenfiddich, Glenlivet, Tomatin – in fact, just about all the Speyside brands. But the island malts like Ardbeg and the Highland brands were uncharted territory.'

'So you'd say Speyside.' Thane drew a satisfied breath. That quiet, mountainous corner of the north-east Highlands was a fairly compact area, even though it seemed to have a distillery at the foot of every hill. 'Can you pin it tighter?'

The little barman shrugged. 'He'd visited a distillery. He didn't tell me where an' I didn't ask. But they were having some kind of big repair job done while he was there – he made a joke about it.'

'All right.' Thane was getting further than he'd hoped. He leaned an elbow on the polished counter. 'While he was here did he talk to anyone, meet anyone?'

'No. Just sat an' drank then went out and got killed.' Cox's thin, sharp face showed his gathering curiosity. 'Look, what's all the fuss about?'

'He was a foreigner.' It wasn't much of a reason, but it seemed to satisfy the man.

'I wondered.' Slightly disappointed, he picked up a cloth and began polishing a glass. 'Everybody seems to want to know about him.'

'Everybody?' Thane raised a questioning eyebrow.

'For one, that reporter who just left.' The barman saw Thane's surprise and grinned. 'He must have passed you on the way out, man. A young bloke, blue anorak, an' long hair. Said he was writing a story to send to some Danish paper.'

'You know him?' asked Thane.

'Never seen him before.' Cox gave a shrug. 'Said his name was Chester, an' that he worked for a

Scandinavian news service over here. But he just wanted to know about the accident – I tol' him to try the reception people in the lobby.'

'Any more like him?' demanded Thane, cursing under his breath.

'No – no reporters. But a big red-faced fellow came in yesterday. He was something to do with insurance.' The little barman winked. 'He was like you, more interested in where Pender had been before he got here. And – uh – generous with his money too.'

'Did he give a name?' asked Thane.

'Kirkson. Didn't tell me who he was working for an' I didn't ask.' Cox paused hopefully. 'Like I said, he was generous.'

'Then he paid for both of us,' said Thane.

He went back out into the lobby, which again was empty apart from the receptionist.

'A newspaperman in a blue anorak – called Chester and asking about Carl Pender,' said Thane curtly. 'Did he talk to you?'

'Yes. Just after you did.' The plump face looked puzzled. 'I suggested he go back into the bar and talk to you, Superintendent. But he walked straight out.'

There was nothing else he could do about it for the moment. Thane left the hotel, got back into the Volkswagen, and drove the short distance to the Firth car rental garage near the airport. The office manager was a brisk young Irishman named O'Brien who didn't waste time.

'We had no problems with Mr Pender.' He turned to a filing cabinet and brought out a booking form. 'He didn't make any arrangements in advance but we got the usual deposit, paid in cash. We gave him a green Chrysler Avenger.'

'Where is it now?'

'Out.' O'Brien checked a wall chart. 'A two-week hire to an American family over on vacation. We cleaned and serviced it first, of course.'

Thane nodded. That meant he could forget the car. 'Did Pender give any indication where he'd be during his week?'

'No.' The young Irishman checked the booking form again. 'But he only clocked up five hundred miles, so he wasn't exactly burning road.' He paused and considered Thane with mild annoyance. 'You know, I've gone through all this already. I mean we had a sergeant in here, asking the same things, even before Mr Pender's accident. Sort of doubling up, aren't you?'

'It happens.' Thane kept his face impassive, but tensed. 'Still, I'll need to check. Who was this sergeant?'

'A plain-clothes man like you, a Sergeant Kirkson,' said O'Brien with dry patience. 'He was quick too – he arrived here only about an hour after Mr Pender returned the car.'

'Kirkson.' Thane winced at the name. 'Did he show you his warrant card?'

'I think so – I'm not sure.' The young Irishman hesitated. 'I mean – well, I don't think I asked.'

'Plenty of people don't,' said Thane. 'What did he look like?'

'Big, red-faced.' O'Brien frowned, trying to be helpful again. 'He said the police had the description of a man driving a green Chrysler they wanted for something that had happened up north, on the A9 road.' He shrugged. 'I told him the same as I've told you, that we didn't know where the car had been. Then I told him the mileage, and he went away.'

'I'll talk to Sergeant Kirkson, if I can find him,' said Thane neutrally. 'Thanks for your time.'

On the way back, he made one more call. It was at the City Mortuary, where an elderly attendant ambled in the lead down a corridor and showed him Carl Pender's body.

Thane stood for a moment, considering the dead man. His face was almost unmarked, a thin, intelligent face yet one that didn't have a single outstanding feature. He shrugged. That had been part of Pender's stock in trade, to be unobtrusive, able to fade into the background.

'He's a mess lower down,' said the attendant helpfully, lifting the mortuary sheet a fraction more. 'See what I mean?'

'Another time,' said Thane, and turned away. He'd achieved all he'd wanted. Carl Pender had been a name, a waiting file. Now he really had been flesh and blood – and it made a difference.

'I've got a new story for you,' said the attendant, following him out. 'Hear the one about the cannibal who didn't like his mother-in-law?'

'His wife told him to just eat the vegetables,' said Thane, and left.

It was dusk when he got back to Millside and left the Volkswagen in the car park. Going up to the C.I.D. room he noted that Dave Andrews had moved into his old office, and smiled a little. The reins had been firmly taken over.

Thane sat at a vacant desk in a corner of the duty room and began using the telephone. He made a series of calls which took half an hour, then sat tight-lipped, considering the results.

There were a few newsmen he knew and could trust. None of them had ever heard of a reporter called Chester or of a Scandinavian news service office in Scotland. The two news agencies which did service the Danish press hadn't bothered to cover Carl Pender's death.

The personnel department at Police Headquarters said there was no Sergeant Kirkson in the force. The traffic department was positive that there was no inquiry going on concerning a green Chrysler – from the A9 north road or anywhere else.

Two fakes, both of them anxious to find out what they could about Carl Pender's last hours, but apparently for different reasons. He swore to himself, crumpled the sheet of paper he'd been using, and tossed it away. Then, suddenly, he realized that the duty room had become oddly quiet. A group of men were standing near the door and one of them came towards him.

'Detective Superintendent, sir –' He got that far, then grinned. 'Pay-off time. We're ready if you are.'

Those law-abiding citizens who lived in the Millside Division of Glasgow wouldn't have approved the thin spread of police cover which protected them that night. It was luck as much as anything that the local neds – Glasgow's label for small-time lawbreakers – kept an equally low profile for once. Most of the time, the easiest way to find a cop, on or off duty, was to visit the saloon bar of the Hydra's Head, a

32

sawdust-on-the-floor establishment located two minutes' walk from Millside Police Station.

Tradition meant Colin Thane bought the first drink
for each new arrival, then stood back – and as the
evening went on he lost count of the number of faces
who came and went. Most were from his own C.I.D.
team, but others were men and women from neigh-
bouring divisions who were equally determined to
come along and slap him on the back.

Halfway through, an improvised barber shop
quartet made up of a police surgeon, a uniformed
inspector and two detective constables got under way
around the battered relic the Hydra's Head management called a piano. While the bar staff worked flat
out and the air grew thick with smoke, the noise
went on.

Then, gradually, there was a general nudging, a
move away from the piano, and a hush. Detective Sergeant MacLeod, the oldest man in the Millside C.I.D.
team, was pushed forward. MacLeod, embarrassed,
made a stumbling attempt at a speech, then quickly
handed over the Division's farewell presentation. It
was a digital watch, with a chrome steel casing and
matching bracelet. The back of the casing had been
engraved 'To the boss, from the Millside team.'

An unaccustomed lump in his throat, Thane
removed his watch and slipped the new digital on his
wrist. Looking at the grinning, friendly faces around,
he cleared his throat.

'I'll treasure this,' he assured them, meaning it.
Then he looked at the watch again and gave a mock
frown. 'But I'll check it against the stolen property
index in the morning.'

Which brought cheers, more attempts at speeches, and another round of drinks.

It was much later before the pay-off party began to die and Thane finally decided he could slip away. Outside, he shivered for a moment in the cold, clear air. The night sky was sprinkled with stars and a chill wind was being funnelled down the street. He'd had more than a shade too much to drink and knew it.

Still, it had been that kind of night. Stopping under a street lamp, he inspected his new watch again, chuckled, and decided he'd walk for a spell before taking a taxi home.

Then, as he started off again, he realized he wasn't alone. A burly figure had stepped out of the shadow of a doorway just ahead, a man with fair, close-cropped hair who wore a long leather jacket and who had a scar twisting one corner of his upper lip. Thane knew him. Tusker Harris was a rogue elephant among neds, the kind who boasted he could chew nails and spit rust.

'Out for some exercise, Tusker?' asked Thane softly, ready for trouble.

'Somethin' like that.' Harris took a shuffling step nearer, hands deep in the pockets of his jacket. 'The word is you're leavin', on your way to the heavy mob.'

'I'm leaving.' Thane left it at that, waiting.

'Aye. From the noise of it, that was one hell of a party they gave you.' Harris gave an embarrassed scowl. 'Anyway, I thought I'd wait an' see you, to say goodbye, like.' He shrugged. 'I've known worse cops.'

Thane smiled. 'The new man plays it straight as well, Tusker. You can spread the word.'

'We'll give him a run.' Harris eyed Thane impassively. 'I'll give you a goodbye present, mister.

34

Someone else seems interested in you. He's in a blue Austin, parked across the street – no lights, an' maybe a hundred yards back. Started up his engine when you came out, but he hasn't moved yet.'

'Thanks,' said Thane quietly. 'How long?'

'Since before I got here. No skin off my nose tellin' you.' Tusker turned and went away.

Thane made a deliberately slow job of lighting a cigarette, then began walking without looking back. Twice, as he passed a shop window, he got a brief, reflected view of the street behind him. The car was there, crawling along, still with no lights, and he couldn't hear the engine.

He reached a street corner where he had to cross. This time he deliberately looked back, and the car had stopped. Impulsively, Thane swung round and started to walk diagonally across the roadway, angling straight towards the stationary Austin.

He hadn't got a quarter of the way when the car engine bellowed, then was slammed into gear. Tyres screaming, the Austin snarled down the street towards him under full acceleration, headlamps blazing to life.

Sheer reflex action sent Thane diving sideways, rolling as he hit the roadway. The car roared past, close enough to spatter him with dirt and gravel.

It kept going. As he scrambled up, Thane was just in time to see the tail lights disappear as it went round the corner in a skidding turn. Then, as the sound of its engine faded, he heard hurrying footsteps and in another moment or so Tusker Harris was standing staring at him.

'That was a pretty daft thing to do.' The big,

scar-faced ned gave a disapproving frown. 'Not your usual style, mister.'

'Maybe.' Thane drew a deep breath. It had happened too fast for anything about the car to really register. 'Did you get its number?'

'Me?' Harris shook his head innocently. 'Not my business, sorry. Uh – any idea why?'

'It could be someone else saying goodbye,' said Thane.

'Could be.' The man rubbed his chin. 'Or maybe hello, eh?'

For the second time, he went away.

Totally sober again, Colin Thane walked a short distance more, then flagged down a passing taxi. On the journey home, he at last got round to glancing at his new watch again – and cursed. The glass had cracked in his fall.

But he could have been dead. Hello or goodbye, somebody didn't like him.

He put the thought out of his mind as the taxi drew up outside his house. Paying the driver, he saw the windows were in darkness and went in quietly.

But, as she'd said, Mary had stayed awake.

Chapter Two

For its public face, the Scottish Crime Squad was openly listed in the Post Office telephone directory with an office in the heart of Glasgow and another located equally openly in Edinburgh. Both were genuine and useful.

But the place that mattered, their operational base, was located south of the River Clyde, a five-minute drive from the city centre across the Kingston Bridge and down the M8 motorway for Greenock.

The outside world saw a fence, trees, grass, and a sign which said Police Training Area. Get past the main gate, drive along a narrow private road, and police horses were usually grazing in a paddock area while the latest intake of Alsatian recruits for Dog Branch training barked impatiently behind their kennel fencing.

The S.C.S. building was at the rear, a modern single-storey structure which might have been a sports pavilion or a golf course clubhouse if it hadn't been for the aerial masts which sprouted from its roof. Part of the building was a technical area – the Crime Squad operated its own, totally separate radio network with its own frequencies and also contained a special

electronic surveillance section with its own sophist-
icated hardware.

Colin Thane rose early that morning with the
remains of a low-grade hangover which his first cup
of breakfast coffee chased away. Then, as Mary cleared
up and got the children out to school, he spent some
time at the kitchen table scribbling a summary of what
had happened the day before.

It wasn't a happy task. He knew enough about the
S.C.S. way of working to be aware they preferred a
low profile on a case until they were ready to move.
If he had become a marked man in the Pender affair
they weren't going to like it.

'Why the frown?' asked Mary, coming back into the
kitchen as he finished. 'First day worries?'

'More a touch of the morning afters,' he lied, fold-
ing the report and tucking it away. Thane hadn't told
her about the car episode. He'd passed off the broken
watch-glass as a spot of horseplay. The new watch
was lying on their bedside table till he could get it
repaired. 'I'd better move.'

'Before I ask awkward questions?' she asked calmly.
'That suit you were wearing looks like you were
rolling around a road. I'll get it cleaned.'

Thane sighed, kissed her, collected his coat, and got
out.

It was just on 9 a.m. when he drove his elderly
station wagon to the main gate at the Scottish Crime
Squad base. The uniformed constable on duty waved
him through and he drove on, past the training area
where some rookie mounties were falling off horses,
then pulled into the car park behind the S.C.S. building. Getting out, he noted a television scanner camera

38

on the roof above but resisted the temptation to give a rude gesture towards the lens.

Feeling like a new schoolboy, he walked over and went in through the glass entrance door. The interior didn't look like a police station, it had more the air of a business office reception area.

'Good morning,' said a smartly dressed woman who sat behind a counter. She was flanked on one side by a small bank of TV monitor screens and on the other by a computer terminal keyboard. 'Superintendent Thane?'

'Yes.' The new title still sounded strange to his ears.

The woman smiled. She wore a wedding ring and her hair showed a first few streaks of grey. Thane guessed she was about his own age. Behind her, a blonde in her twenties stopped thumping a typewriter for a moment and gave him a glance of casual interest.

'Go straight through. Commander Hart's door is third on the left. Superintendent Maxwell is with him.' The woman's smile stayed friendly. 'I'm Maggie Fyffe, the commander's secretary and general dogsbody. Anything you need, let me know.'

A telephone at her elbow buzzed and she turned to answer it. Thane went along the corridor, passing a couple of men who were going out. They were young, they wore grubby jeans and sweatshirts with knitted wool jackets, and both needed a shave. One murmured a greeting as they went by. The last time Thane had seen him he had been an immaculately dressed detective constable in Central Division.

The third door on the left had a small metal plate with the word 'Commander'. Thane pressed the bellpush beside it and an 'Enter' sign lit up. He went in, closed the door quietly behind him, and faced the man who was his new boss.

'So you survived your pay-off.' A tall, thin, dark-haired man rose from behind a desk and crossed the room to give him a firm handshake. Commander Hart was in his late forties, a man with high cheekbones and a lined, almost sad-eyed face. 'Welcome aboard. Tom Maxwell you know.'

Thane nodded to Maxwell, who was standing in the background. Then he faced Hart again.

It was the first time they'd met. Jack Hart, he knew, was a detective chief superintendent who had been an area C.I.D. commander in the Ayrshire sector of Strathclyde before he'd taken over the Scottish Crime Squad. Apart from a large, pleasantly furnished office with a picture-window view towards the nearby motorway, the job gave him a degree of operational autonomy few other policemen could claim – or would want. He made his own decisions on most things and individual chief constables seldom tried to interfere.

'We'll make a civilized start,' said Hart after a moment's mutual scrutiny. He gestured towards his desk, where a coffee pot and cups were waiting on a tray. 'Find a chair, then help yourself.'

They settled down, Hart behind his desk, Maxwell and Thane on the other side. Waiting for the others, then pouring his own coffee, Thane decided it wasn't chance that Hart's desk was positioned so that the sunlight streaming in through the window framed the squad commander like a halo. But that didn't make him any kind of angel.

He got proof of that a moment later.

'Patience doesn't seem to be one of your virtues,'

said Hart suddenly, sitting back. 'I hear you've been sniffing on your own around the Pender business – Drug Squad and Criminal Intelligence for a start.' He frowned. 'I don't necessarily like it, large feet trampling around. Remember that.'

'Yes, sir.' Thane drew a deep breath and took the handwritten report from his inside pocket. 'I – well, I think you'd better see this.'

Silently Hart took the report, produced a pair of metal-framed spectacles, and began reading. Halfway through, he glanced up sharply, his thin, lined face wiped clean of expression. Then, saying nothing, he continued reading. When he finished, he took a deliberate gulp of coffee before he spoke.

'You know nothing more about the car that almost rammed you?'

Thane shook his head

'You realize what it maybe means?' Grimly, Hart slid the report across his desk to Maxwell.

'That someone knows I'm interested in Pender.' Thane saw no sense in trying to dodge the issue. 'I'm sorry.'

'Sorrow we can do without.' Hart spoke almost absently, drumming his thin, long fingers on his desk, lost in thought. Then he glanced at Maxwell. 'Tom?'

'We can't be sure.' Maxwell had finished his own skim through the report. 'But it looks that way. And – well, if they got his name at the hotel it wouldn't be too hard to find out he was Millside-based, or had been. So they could pick him up there.'

'Yes.' Hart gave a surprising chuckle. 'Well, what the hell difference does it really make this time? All right, Thane, the rest of it paid off – the Speyside whisky lead, your phoney reporter, and equally

41

phoney cop. That's all new, all worth having.' A glint of cold humour showed in his eyes. 'And if these people are interested in you, then that means we can always use you as live bait, which may give even more. Our sacrificial goat.' Hart found the idea amusing. The crisis was over. 'We'll start checking on the Speyside angle, this distillery with a repair programme. And there's another possible lead, one you don't know about. Francey Dunbar, one of our sergeants, came up with it – he's being assigned to you anyway, so I'll leave him to tell you about it.'

'He's on it now,' murmured Maxwell. He glanced sideways at Hart. 'Maybe we should warn him about Francey, sir.'

'Yes.' Hart gave a long sigh. 'Francey Dunbar can be an awkward character. He enjoys it. But he's also a good cop – don't judge him straight off by the way he acts.' He settled back in his chair again, and for a moment became almost benevolent. 'That brings me to the standard lecture, Thane. You get it just once – any man who needs it again is out.'

He paused and Thane nodded, wondered if he should say anything, then saw Maxwell give a small, warning headshake.

'It goes like this,' said Hart soberly. 'I've men and women in this squad from every police force in the country. They're hand-picked, they're hard-nosed when they need to be – but I don't allow anyone to go out thinking he or she is some kind of supercop. They're not, and I've no time for animals with big fists.' Suddenly, he switched direction. 'How did you run your divisional team?'

'For results.' It sounded inadequate, but Thane

42

wasn't sure where to go from there. 'It seemed to work. Nobody ever stuck a knife in my back.'

'The same applies here – results,' said Hart. His voice took on a sardonic edge. 'Our people don't come out of a chocolate box, unless that's needed. If a man reckons he has a better chance of getting results by not shaving, not washing, or dressing like a tramp that's his decision – as long as he remembers he stays inside the law.' He slapped one hand on the desk. 'That doesn't mean we throw discipline out the window. But our brand is elastic at the edges.'

The lecture had ended. Tom Maxwell immediately cleared his throat.

'I'll show you your office,' he volunteered.

Hart nodded approval and Thane followed Maxwell as he limped out of the room. They went down a side corridor, then Maxwell opened a door and stood back.

'This is it,' he said.

It was a modest-sized office, sparsely furnished, and the window looked out on the car park. But it had wall-to-wall carpet – superintendents rated carpets. Thane went in, tried the chair behind the desk, and noted the dark red envelope folder labelled 'Carl Pender, Deceased' which was waiting for him.

'There are a couple of things Jack Hart didn't get round to mentioning,' said Maxwell, leaning in the doorway. 'One is that you're third in command – if Hart and I get knocked off in a car crash or anything, you're running the show. The other is what I said yesterday about paperwork. I meant it. Thank the Lord, we're supposed to catch villains, not beat them to death with notebooks.' He peered around. 'Anything else you need? If there is, Maggie Fyffe will fix it.'

'I met her,' said Thane, checking the empty desk drawers. 'She seems a friendly dragon lady.'

'Maggie is a widow.' Maxwell gave a minimal shrug. 'Her husband was a cop who got shot in the guts trying to stop a bank hold-up, then took three years to die. So – well, she fixes things.' He eased himself off the doorpost. 'I'll leave you to settle in. Francey Dunbar shouldn't be long.'

The door closed. Thane sat back, enjoying the feel of the chair sagging comfortably beneath his weight. It had a swivel. He swung in it a couple of times like a child with a new toy, then checked the last of the desk drawers. It had been stocked for him, from pens and paper clips to an S.C.S. roster list and a typed three-page memo on basic procedures.

He read it through quickly, found nothing that surprised him, then turned to the envelope folder on Carl Pender. The main item to interest him was a copy of a long telex message received from the Danish police. Carl Pender did have a small bookselling business in Copenhagen, but for more than a year he had been on their list as a suspected drug traffic courier – suspected, because there had never been enough evidence to charge him.

The dry, factual wordage sketched a picture of a man who frequently travelled abroad, who had plenty of underworld contacts, and who seldom took chances.

Which didn't give much to go on. Closing the folder, Thane lit a cigarette, then glanced up as he heard a light tap on the door and it swung open.

'Sergeant Dunbar, sir,' said the man who came ambling in. He was slim, just over medium height, and in his twenties, with a mop of jet black hair, a strong nose, and a wide, humorous mouth framed by a long, thin straggle of a moustache. One foot eased the door shut behind him, then he stood eyeing Thane with interest as he added laconically, 'The boss says I'm working with you.'

Thane nodded. His new sergeant wore an old Donegal tweed safari jacket with a grey rolled-neck shirt, tan whipcord slacks, and scuffed leather boots. A heavy silver identity bracelet, the name-tab blank, hung loose on his right wrist. It was an outfit which, like its owner, looked both casual and practical.

'I heard, Sergeant.' He considered the slight, rhythmic movement of Dunbar's jaws. 'Having a late breakfast?'

'Just gum, sir.' Unconcerned, Dunbar let his eyes stray to Thane's cigarette. 'I stopped smoking. But – uh –' With an air of outraged innocence, he removed the gum and carefully dropped it into Thane's waste basket. 'Sorry.'

'Francey.' Thane's voice stayed mild. 'Let's start off right, eh? Chew gum if you want, walk on your hands if you feel inclined. But when it comes to work, stay in line or I'll personally kick your backside so hard it jams your earholes.'

A slow, delighted grin slid across Dunbar's face. He straightened a degree or two.

'Sounds painful, sir,' he said cheerfully. 'I won't forget.'

'Then sit down.' Thane pointed towards a chair. 'Commander Hart said you'd come up with something.'

'It looks that way.' Dunbar rested his hands on a chair-back, but remained standing. He chewed an

45

edge of moustache for a moment. 'Do I start at the beginning?'

'Yes. But forget the frills.'

'The way it happened was chance,' said Dunbar. 'You see, last night I was – well, out with this bird, a British Airways stewardess. She's London-based, but she does an overnight here now and again. When that happens –' He saw the warning glint in Thane's eyes and moved on hastily. 'Anyway, she told me the airlines have had problems at Glasgow for the last ten days or so. Some of the maintenance crews are on a go-slow, and a fair scatter of flights out have had to be cancelled. Which leaves the airlines chasing passengers by phone, rescheduling their flights. It's still happening.'

'Go on.' Thane stubbed his cigarette, his eyes narrowing. 'You checked Pender's flight?'

'This morning, first thing. I – uh – well, what she said didn't click straight off,' admitted Dunbar apologetically. 'When Pender flew in from Copenhagen he did the usual, confirmed his seat reservation for the flight home. The airline wanted a phone number where they could reach him or leave a message in case they had to reschedule and he gave them one.'

'Up north?' Thane tensed. 'Francey, if we've got that –'

'No, it's here, in Glasgow. A girl, a woman anyway,' Dunbar told him, leaning his weight on the chair. 'The number is listed for a Miss Marion Cooper, at 200 Griffon Street, and I think I know it, a block of rented apartments.' He paused hopefully. 'Want me to go out and have a sniff?'

'Get a car,' said Thane, rising. 'We're both going.'

*   *   *

46

They were on their way a few minutes later, Francey Dunbar driving. The car was an unmarked, distinctly mud-splashed blue Ford Cortina. The badge on the tail said it was a basic model but the acceleration made that a lie. In the same way there was no visible radio aerial, but a ten-frequency transmitter set of a kind Thane hadn't seen before was slotted into the shelf on the passenger side.

'We do our own thing mostly,' said Dunbar, gesturing towards the radio. 'Low-band transmission with scrambler facility so the punter with a home v.h.f. set can't eavesdrop. And the boss doesn't like clean cars – claims people notice them. We just put them through a car wash now and again to make sure the colours haven't changed.' He kept his eyes on the road. 'Like that old station wagon you've got?'

'It runs on faith,' said Thane dryly. 'Faith and the family budget.'

'Well, I told Maggie we'd hang on to this one.' Dunbar slid the Ford through a set of traffic lights, turning right. They were heading into the city through a mixture of red sandstone tenements, old villas, and the occasional cinema turned bingo hall. 'I've got a motor cycle at home – a 750 c.c. Honda. Don't get to use it much, though.'

'Where's home?' asked Thane, watching the speedometer. 'A racetrack?'

'No, sir.' Dunbar eased back on the accelerator. 'Near Edinburgh – my folks still live there.' He was checking the streets as they went past. 'Next one is ours.'

They turned into Griffon Street, a long, curving avenue which began as terraced houses then changed to modern apartment blocks.

'We want the first of the new blocks, I think.'
Dunbar frowned ahead, bringing the Ford down to a
crawl and keeping it close to the kerb. 'I used to go
with a girl out this way. A brunette and –'

'Pull in,' ordered Thane, cutting the reminiscence
short. He pointed towards an elderly postman who
was walking on the pavement across the street, sorting a bundle of letters. 'Try the local Royal Mail. See
if he knows Marion Cooper.'

Francey Dunbar stopped the car, got out, and
trotted across the road. Thane watched as the black-
haired sergeant, a smile on his face, talked to the
somewhat startled postman for a couple of minutes.
Then they parted, the postman looking slightly
puzzled. Coming back across the road, Dunbar
slipped back into his seat behind the wheel.

'He knows her.' He unwrapped a stick of gum as he
spoke, popped it into his mouth, and began chewing
energetically. 'She's early twenties, blonde but plain,
English accent. Moved in about three or four months
back and lives alone – or that's how it looks. She
doesn't get many letters and he reckons the ones
that come are mostly bills. And he thinks she probably
has a night job somewhere. The first mail delivery is
always about 10 a.m. and she usually answers the
door in a dressing gown.'

'Lucky postman,' said Thane. 'Doesn't she have a
letter box?'

Dunbar shrugged. 'The lady got a load of registered
packages for a spell. She had to sign for them.'

'Does he remember what they were like?' asked
Thane, frowning.

'Big, not too heavy – they were usually marked
"Fragile", sir.'

'So Post Office sorters know to bounce them off the nearest concrete.' Thane spoke half-aloud. 'Francey, how much small glassware would you need if you were setting up a laboratory? The kind you didn't want anyone to know about?'

Francey Dunbar's eyes widened. He started to open his mouth, closed it again, and nodded.

They parked outside 200 Griffon Street, a plain, modern seven-storey filing cabinet for people, which owed more to geometry than architecture, went in, and checked a directory board on the wall beside the lifts in the terrazzo-floored entrance hall. Marion Cooper's name was listed for Apartment F on the third floor and they took the lift up. It was frontal attack stuff and Thane knew it. But his mind was made up. He had this one lead and he had to use it, then watch the results.

The lift opened on to a carpeted corridor. Marion Cooper's door was the last on the left, painted cream with a small spyhole set in the middle.

Thane reached for the doorbell.

'Sir –' Francey Dunbar stopped him sharply.

He saw why at the same moment, the fine splintering of wood around the door lock area on an otherwise immaculately painted woodwork. Dunbar touched the door, pushed slightly with his fingertips, and it opened a fraction. He glanced at Thane, pushed again, and the door swung wider.

They went in. Three open doors led off a small, square hall. The nearest was into a bedroom. Drawers lay open and a wardrobe had only some coathangers left on its rail. Thane crossed to the next doorway.

49

'Hell,' he said quietly, and heard Francey Dunbar suck a quick intake of breath.

The body of a man lay in a pool of blood on the floor just inside the doorway. A towel covered his head. Stooping, Thane lifted the towel and wished he hadn't. The man had been shot in the face and the exit wound had blown away part of the back of his head.

Wincing, Thane looked past the dead man into a modest-sized living room. Drawers in a sideboard lay open and the room looked as though it had been systematically searched – or emptied.

Francey Dunbar had gone when Thane turned. He found the dark-haired sergeant when he went to the remaining doorway, which led into a small kitchen.

'Bathroom that way, sir,' said Dunbar, pointing to a door leading off the kitchen. His voice had a hoarse edge. 'That's the lot, and it's empty, like here. Any idea who – well, who that was back there?'

'He didn't tell me,' said Thane wryly. He looked at Dunbar, whose face was pale. 'Sometimes they come messy.'

'I've seen worse.' Dunbar shrugged. 'That doesn't mean I have to like them. What now?'

'I'll look him over and check the living room,' said Thane. 'You close the front door, then look around the rest of the place.'

Dunbar nodded and went off. Going back to the living room, Thane bent over the dead man again. He was about thirty, medium height and build, with light brown hair, blue eyes, and a small gold earring in the lobe of one ear. His clothing, a grey suit with dark blue shirt and matching tie, hadn't come from a bargain basement.

Skirting the pool of blood, noting how it had almost

dried into the carpeting, Thane examined the suit pockets. He found cigarettes and a lighter, a wallet holding about fifty pounds, and a few minor items. Then, as he opened the jacket, he sat back on his heels with a grunt.

The dead man wore a shoulder holster, but it was empty. Metal clanked on metal as Thane shifted his grip on the cloth and he found a compact forged steel jemmy and a penlight torch in an inside pocket. There was nothing else, nothing to help him put a name to the body beside him.

He put everything back where it had come from, fastened the jacket again, and looked around for the gun that belonged to the holster. There was no sign of it. Shrugging, he rose and made a slow inspection of the rest of the room, noting a few small smears of dried blood on the carpet as if feet had carried them along. Then, skirting the bloodstain again, he went back through to the kitchen.

Francey Dunbar was there, opening cupboards. He glanced around and shook his head as Thane entered.

'Cleaned out, sir. Clothes, papers, everything – this woman really did a removal job.' His nose wrinkled. 'There's a stale smell in this place.'

Thane sniffed the air, caught a sour smell, and nodded. 'Drains, probably. Didn't she leave anything else?'

'Just a few cans of food in here and an opened bottle of whisky in that end cupboard.' Dunbar had recovered enough to grin. 'The Cooper woman must like liquor. There's another bottle, an empty, in the rubbish bucket.'

Thane nodded absently, then a sudden wisp of a possibility made him more interested.

'Malt whisky, or a blend?' he asked.

'Uh – I'm not sure,' admitted Dunbar, surprised.

'Show me,' ordered Thane.

Puzzled, Dunbar opened a cupboard and pointed. Thane looked closely at the half-empty bottle and its red-and-white label.

'Glendirk,' said Dunbar helpfully. 'It's a Speyside malt.'

'I can read, Sergeant,' agreed Thane frostily. 'And the other bottle?'

Dunbar sighed openly, crossed to the rubbish bucket, and looked in.

'The same. Does it matter, sir?'

'It might.' Thane saw his sergeant's blank lack of understanding. 'There's a strong chance that Carl Pender was up around Speyside, and he talked about visiting a distillery – these might tie in.' He gestured at the bottle in the cupboard. 'You don't find Glendirk in your average off-licence, Francey. Most of it is exported.'

'I see.' Dunbar stuck his hands in his pockets, not particularly impressed. 'Uh – what about the way things are here?'

Thane shrugged. 'That's no ordinary housebreaker through there. He's well dressed, he's wearing a shoulder holster – I think he came looking, the same way we did.'

'He ran out of luck,' said Dunbar gravely, then frowned. 'Well, if it was the Cooper woman who shot him, she may have decided to bail out but she certainly didn't panic. Packing up and emptying this place would take an hour or two.'

'She probably had help.' Thane was trying to put the rest of it together in his mind. From the way the pool of blood around the dead man had dried the shooting had happened the previous night or earlier. Yet even more important was why it had happened. If Marion Cooper was a link to the amphetamine operation, then the break-in meant yet again that the police weren't the only people interested. He chewed his lip for a moment, then came back to practicalities. 'Francey, I'm going to leave you to tidy things here.'

'I thought that was coming,' said Dunbar wryly. 'Do I get to know where you'll be?'

'At Strathclyde Headquarters, with the forensic mob. I'll take the car and you can thumb a lift back to base – I'll see you there.' Thane paused, assembling a quick mental check-list. 'Better phone Commander Hart for a start. Tell him about this and the whisky bottles.'

'Then let the local troops know?' asked Dunbar, feeding a stick of chewing gum into his mouth.

'Once you've cleared it with Hart.' Thane nodded. 'When the divisional team gets here, I want a priority fingerprinting job on our body. They'd better wire a set to London as well as making their own try at matching them against the usual Scottish punters on file.'

'London.' Dunbar raised an eyebrow. 'Why?'

'A hunch, that's all,' admitted Thane. 'Another thing, Francey, talk to the neighbours. Find out what they know about Marion Cooper, any gossip that's going.'

'Right. But there may not be much – not in a block where a man can get shot and lie behind an unlocked door for God knows how long.'

'It's called respecting privacy,' said Thane dryly. He took the car keys from Dunbar and left.

53

Francey Dunbar sighed as he heard the front door close. He looked thoughtfully at the whisky bottle in the cupboard, took out his handkerchief, used it to grip the bottle and avoid leaving prints, found a glass and poured himself a stiff drink. He gulped it down with scant respect, washed and dried the glass, returned the whisky bottle to the cupboard, then set to work.

Matthew Amos, assistant director at the Strathclyde police forensic laboratory, was in an ebullient mood when Thane got there. That usually meant he'd just annoyed someone.

'Welcome to our humble workshop,' he said breezily, waving a hand towards the main laboratory area. It was a clinical place of white walls and microscopes, unidentifiable apparatus and quietly clicking electronics, the effect somewhat marred by a couple of girlie posters seized in a porn shop raid and promptly claimed as 'study material' by Amos and his team. Amos grinned at Thane and added, 'How's the newest recruit to the heavy mob? Command and we'll think about it – negotiate, anyway.'

'Having a happy day?' asked Thane mildly.

He rubbed along fairly well with Matt Amos, a slim, bearded civilian who always wore a dazzling line in bow ties and who made almost a hobby out of annoying authority – like the time when after a quarrel with an assistant chief constable he'd had the executive corridor washroom closed for a week on the pretext he'd grown suspicious germ cultures from its walls. But Amos was no clown. He had come to the job from a top university research team, not for money but because he said he wanted to get back into the real world again.

'Not happy, more productive.' Amos stuck his hands into the pockets of his white laboratory coat and winked. 'Won myself a new friend. We've just told a cop in Argyll that what he thought was blood on a knife is dried fruit juice – ruined his case. So, how can we hinder you?'

'The amphetamine samples,' said Thane. 'You're supposed to be working on them.'

'You drew that one?' Matt Amos gave a wince of genuine sympathy. 'We've finished – more or less, anyway. No report typed up, but I can tell you about them. Hold on.'

He left Thane, threaded a way through the work benches where several of his staff were busy, and spoke for a moment to a slim, raven-haired girl who was standing beside some bulky glass apparatus and a flaming gas jet. The girl glanced round in Thane's direction, smiled and nodded. She had good looks, dazzling white teeth, and a figure which even her white coat couldn't conceal. Apparently satisfied, Amos slapped her casually on the rump and came back.

'She's new,' said Thane.

'Stole her from a drug company,' said Amos. 'She has a brain like a computer, but she makes lousy coffee.' He led Thane through to his private office, where magazine pictures of Karl and Groucho Marx glared at each other from opposite walls. Closing the door, Amos thumbed an invitation. 'Sit down.'

Thane took a chair, though he first had to dump some scientific journals on the floor. Amos contented himself with his desk-top, sitting with his legs swing-ing, which exposed a pair of canary yellow socks.

'How's Phil Moss?' he asked.

'Recovering. He's declared war on the nursing profession.'

'Great.' Amos chuckled. 'To work then, Colin. I'm not going to waste my time or yours explaining what we've done. Let's face it, you wouldn't understand half I said, and you don't have to – fair enough?'

Thane nodded. Amos had a dry liking to refer to himself as a simple mechanic, but when it came to his job he was a total expert who only dealt in estab-lished, clinical fact and ice-cold logic.

'Right.' The humour had gone from Amos's voice. 'You know about amphetamines – how they're used, that sort of thing?'

'The basics,' agreed Thane. 'Enough for now.'

He'd fleshed out his knowledge in his Drug Squad visit the day before. Amphetamines meant anti-depressants, boosters, to the medical world, though they had other uses. Doctors had at one time pre-scribed them by the cart-load for legitimate patients, then had become more careful.

But on the drug scene amphetamine had other names. Names like speed and bennies or jolly beans – to be sniffed or swallowed or injected, or sometimes used as a cocktail mix with LSD. To an addict, 'speed' meant kicks and action with a feeling of power, which manifested itself gradually to the rest of humanity as aggressive hostility blending into suspicion and downright paranoia while the dosage built up and physical health began to collapse.

'Wake-ups – that's what we called them when I was a kid in the university mill,' mused Amos. His eyes grew distant at the memory. 'They got a hell of a lot of us through our finals, but that was before the speed freaks, the needle idiots, the kids looking for kicks and ending up wrecking themselves.' He paused, and changed as if a switch had been thrown. 'Right. The late, apparently unlamented Carl Pender was carrying high-grade amphetamine, about as near as you can get to one hundred per cent pure.'

'Then the maker knows his business?' asked Thane.

'Knows it?' Matt Amos gave a snort. 'Hell, the product is as good as you'll get from any legitimate manufacturer. Out on the street, a dealer could cut it fifty-fifty with chalk or any old rubbish and the customers would still think it dreamland stuff.'

'Fine,' said Thane. 'So now all I've got to do is find where it came from. Matt, can you tie it in with the chemicals that were stolen in Edinburgh?'

'Yes and no.' The assistant director retreated behind an immediate shield of professional caution. He came down off his desk, raked in a wire basket, and brought out some sheets of paper covered in scribbled notes. 'I can tell you what they're doing. They're converting phenylacetic acid, passing it in solution under nitrogen and over treated pumice stone – that gives them benzyl methyl ketone, and the rest of it is downhill from there.' He paused and shrugged. 'I've got the shopping list from the Edinburgh raid. It started off with six drums of phenylacetic acid, thirty kilograms per drum, then just about everything else they'd need. But the stuff doesn't pop out with any tag on it that says "Made in Scotland".'

'I wasn't expecting a tartan wrapper,' protested Thane. 'But –'

'But nothing,' said Amos grimly. 'Look, there are plenty of different cook-book recipes for amphetamine production – you can find them in the science section of your local public library if you know where to look. All my people can positively say is the recipe used for Pender's samples needed the main ingredients stolen in Edinburgh.' He drew a deep breath and tossed the notes aside. 'I've come across other underground factories, but this is the best. They've got a damned good chemist and a first-class production line.'

'A good chemist, good planning, and some good contacts when they came up with Pender.' Thane knew that when Amos dug his heels in they stayed that way. 'What kind of a base would they need?'

'A house, a small garage – hell, even a cellar. They'd need a certain amount of equipment, but nothing tremendously complicated. They'd have only one problem. I'll tell you about that in a minute.' A slight grin on his bearded face, Amos flicked a switch on his desk intercom, waited for an answer, then said briskly, 'My love, bring in our little gift. Don't bother wrapping it.' He closed the switch and faced Thane again. 'So, what's next on your list?'

'Suppose they're in full production,' said Thane. 'What kind of take-home pay will they have at the end of the day?'

'Better than us,' said Amos wryly. 'Raw, the Edinburgh chemicals were worth about six thousand pounds. Converted, the end product will be twenty-two kilograms of amphetamine worth maybe three million pounds on the street – as producers selling in bulk, they'll make about a million. It depends on the kind of deal they do.'

There was a knock on the door as he finished. It opened, and the raven-haired girl from the laboratory came in. She carried a small glass jar, covered with a lid.

'Thanks, Betty.' Amos took the glass jar from the girl, then considered her carefully, frowning. 'All right, I give up. Exactly how little are you wearing under that lab coat?'

'Enough. I've got a date after work and I don't want my dress crushed,' she declared calmly. 'Don't worry, decency rules.'

'Hanging on by its fingertips,' murmured Amos, and sighed. 'I'm not complaining. Just don't get arrested.'

'That's about the least worry I've got around here,' she retorted and went out.

Grinning, Amos beckoned Thane over beside him as the door closed.

'Take a sniff of this,' he ordered, removing the lid from the jar. 'Not too much.'

Thane saw a light brownish powder, sniffed obediently, then recoiled from the foul, rank odour which filled his nostrils. It was like a sickening blend of dried urine and soured wine.

'Distinctive,' said Amos sympathetically. 'But useful – that's why I had it made up. That's the stink from the halfway stage of amphetamine production. Like someone heated an abandoned sewer – and it lingers.'

'Wait.' Thane stopped him as he made to replace the lid.

He took another cautious sniff. The same cloying smell, much fainter but totally distinctive, was the one he'd blamed on the drains at Marion Cooper's place in Griffon Street.

'Met it already?' asked Amos, watching him.

'Maybe. I think so.'

'It'll cling to clothes for months.' Amos put the lid on the jar and set it down. 'Where?'

'In an apartment block, this morning. The occupier has skipped and left a dead man behind,' Thane said shortly. 'Some of it will be coming your way.'

'Some of it always does,' sighed Amos. 'But that certainly wasn't your factory – the neighbours would have gone crazy. No, more likely the smell got there on a pair of overalls or a bundle of washing.' He took a few paces around the room, then stopped and faced Thane again. Suddenly he was totally serious, his voice almost harsh. 'Colin, some people think amphetamines are kids' stuff. They're not. Have you any idea how much misery this outfit can cause if they market?'

'I can guess.' Thane took out his cigarettes, offered them, then lit one himself as Amos shook his head. 'You say it's high quality. If the right people knew, what would the competition be like?'

'To get it?' Amos shrugged. 'Fierce – no holds barred.'

Thane said nothing. But it fitted, it might be part of the answer. An answer worth three million pounds that could attract any number of vultures.

Unless he got there first.

Chapter Three

A light breeze was scattering leaves across the car park when Colin Thane returned to the Scottish Crime Squad office. He parked the Ford, walked across the sunlit yard, and was hailed by Maggie Fyffe as soon as he entered the building.

'Two phone messages for you,' she said briskly, coming out from behind her reception counter to intercept him. 'Sergeant Dunbar called, and the censored version is he's on his way back here now. The other was from a friend of yours called Moss. He wants to see you as soon as possible.'

Thane raised an eyebrow. 'Did he say why?'

'No.' She shook her head. 'A woman made the call for him. That's all she said.'

'Thanks.' Absently he noted that Maggie Fyffe had good legs, good enough to belong to a woman half her age. 'Is the commander in?'

'It's Wednesday,' she said flatly, then seemed to remember he was the new boy. 'The commander has a weekly lunch meeting in Edinburgh on Wednesday, branch office style. But Tom Maxwell wants to see you. I'll let him know you're back.'

Thanking her, Thane went along the corridor towards his new office. On the way, he reached a door marked 'Duty Room'. It was lying open and he looked in on a large room which held the usual layout of desks and telephones. But the maps on the walls covered all of Scotland and only two of the desks were occupied. A dark-haired girl wearing jeans and a sweater sat reading a newspaper. A man dressed in black motor-cycle leathers was humming to himself and had a large mirror propped up in front of him. He tugged at his long, dirty fair hair, and it was a wig which came away in his hands. His own hair was short and ginger.

'Sir?' He saw Thane in the mirror and turned with friendly but guarded curiosity. 'Can I help?'

'Just prowling, finding my way,' said Thane.

He nodded to the girl, who had lowered her newspaper, and backed out. Reaching his office, he settled gladly behind the desk and gave a wry grimace. This wasn't Millside Division and he'd have to get used to the differences, which weren't just detail aspects like the total absence of uniformed staff or the way in which there were no cells for prisoners, who were always handed on to someone else.

As a group, Commander Hart's team would probably have laughed like drains if they'd been called any kind of elite. But all of them – even Maggie Fyffe – had a special kind of relaxed assurance that held its own close understanding and left him an outsider who still had to prove himself.

With, as things stood, an uphill task.

He sighed. Then, still puzzled by Moss's message, he reached for the telephone and dialled the Western Infirmary number. When he got through, he asked for Moss's ward.

'Staff Nurse,' said the brisk voice which answered.

'Nurse Blair?' He recognized the voice as Moss's current enemy and smiled slightly. 'My name is Thane, I've had a message from –'

'From our Mr Moss.' Staff Nurse Blair finished it for him in a resigned way. 'I know. He insisted I call you.'

'Anything wrong?' asked Thane.

'Not with him.' A tendril of doubt crept into the woman's voice. 'But he has some odd notion about another of our patients. I – well, I don't know, it seems impossible to me.'

'Phil Moss is a good cop,' said Thane quietly.

'I guessed that,' she said. 'He just happens to be impossible in every other way. But –'

'Tell him I'll be over,' said Thane. 'And you've got my sympathy.'

He said goodbye and hung up.

Sitting back, he took Matt Amos's sample bottle from his pocket, sniffed the contents again, then replaced the lid and put the bottle in his top drawer. A potential three million pounds' worth of amphetamine, two dead men, and a woman who had vanished – it made one hell of an introductory package.

The door opened, and Tom Maxwell limped in.

'Bless this house,' said Maxwell sardonically, propping himself against the wall. 'Settling in?'

'That's one way of putting it,' said Thane flatly.

'Then I'll brighten your life,' said Maxwell. 'Glendirk distillery was having some urgent pipework repairs carried out last week. Production was pretty well stopped. Your whisky bottle notion paid off.' He grinned. 'Incidentally, what did you do to Francey Dunbar? He's really working on this one.'

'Threatened him with grievous bodily harm.' Thane

63

chewed his lip, thinking. 'What about our dead house-breaker?'

'Fingerprinted, and a priority tag on getting them matched,' nodded Maxwell. 'Same with the bullet that killed him – just in case.'

'Thanks.' Thane knew he should have thought of that one himself. 'But the rest of it comes down to the Cooper woman and this distillery.'

'Right,' agreed Maxwell cheerfully. 'That's what the boss said. So he wants you to head up to Speyside this afternoon.'

'Front door style, or quietly?' asked Thane, frowning.

'Your choice.' Tom Maxwell made his way to the window and looked out towards the busy motorway. 'Glendirk distillery is at a village called Crossglen, not far from Aviemore. Maggie Fyffe is booking you and Francey Dunbar into the local hotel and we've a contact on Speyside who'll meet you there. He's Angus Russell, a freelance photographer – you can trust him, we've used him before.'

'And the local police?'

'Their Force Headquarters will know you're working in their area – routine courtesy style. The locals won't know until you need them. As far as the hotel is concerned, Maggie will book you in as a couple of visiting tourists – that's thin, but it'll do for starters.' Maxwell turned to face him. 'Now, what did you get from the forensic mob?'

'That it's a three-million-pound deal.'

Maxwell winced and listened grimly to the rest.

'Anything more to add to the misery?' he asked as Thane finished.

'We've got competition,' said Thane. 'Someone else

has been trying hard to find them and knew Carl Pender was here. Now,' he shrugged, 'I think they're still trying, which explains the dead man in the Cooper woman's apartment. But they're not acting like buyers who want to put in a bid. It's more like they want to take over.'

'There's a happy thought,' said Maxwell. 'We could end up in the middle of a war.'

He limped out and it was another half-hour before Francey Dunbar arrived. Something was annoying him and he didn't attempt to hide it.

'Maggie says we're going north,' he said, scowling across the desk at Thane.

'She's right,' agreed Thane. 'If that causes havoc with your sex life, too bad.'

'Not tonight,' said Dunbar indignantly. 'I'm due at a Police Federation meeting – I'm the Squad delegate.'

'Democracy should survive,' said Thane. He brought the forensic lab bottle from his desk drawer and slid it across. 'Sit down. Smell this.'

Puzzled, indignation giving way to curiosity, Dunbar obeyed, removed the lid, and sniffed. His broad nostrils wrinkled in disgust, then understanding dawned.

'So it wasn't the drains?'

'Half-cooked amphetamine.' Thane closed the bottle and put it away. 'Maybe it was there in transit, but that's incidental.' He told Dunbar the rest and saw the last of the dark-haired sergeant's indignation vanish. 'That's my end, Francey. What happened with you?'

'Bits and pieces, sir.' Dunbar sucked a corner of his thin moustache, as if deciding where to start. 'I stayed in the Cooper woman's apartment for a spell. The divisional team turned up with a brand new police surgeon, still hedging his bets. You show him a body with half its head blown away and all he'll say is the apparent cause of death is a gunshot wound, but he reckons it happened around midnight last night.'

'Midnight.' Thane repeated the word thoughtfully, a slender possibility edging into his mind. 'Francey, does Marion Cooper own a car?'

Dunbar nodded. 'There's a caretaker for the block and I talked to him. He says she has a blue Austin.' He paused cautiously. 'I heard something about a car like that nearly clipping you last night.'

'Then maybe they went home and found a visitor?' Thane chewed his lip, knowing it fitted. 'What about her neighbours?'

Dunbar shrugged. 'I tried the ones who were home. That place is one big hen-roost of women on their own, most of them at work during the day –'

'Then make sure someone has another try, later,' said Thane impatiently. 'What's the gossip about her?'

'Only a few had even met her,' grimaced Dunbar. 'None had ever been over her doorstep, though one or two had tried.' He shook his head. 'Seems she was away a lot too, sometimes a week or more at a time – the polite ones thought she must be some kind of sales rep.'

'Any mention of men?'

'Footsteps in the night stuff,' shrugged Dunbar. 'Different men, sometimes more than one at a time, usually late at night – or so they claim. But no clear descriptions. It's like a kind of local etiquette – don't look, it might be someone else's husband. And the caretaker wasn't much use, apart from what he said about the car. As far as he was concerned, Marion

Cooper was just another tenant, rent paid cash in advance.'

'All right.' Thane sighed and glanced at his: wristwatch. It was almost one o'clock. 'It's still my first day, so I'll buy you lunch – as long as you don't mention that damned Federation meeting.'

Dunbar gave a surprised grin, nodded, and hauled himself to his feet.

They ate at a small restaurant a little way down the road. The food was reasonable and so was the bill, even if the beer was lukewarm. It was also quiet enough for them to talk, but they stayed clear of anything to do with work. Francey Dunbar worked himself up into a brief, patriotic fervour about Scotland's football chances, then listened with dry amusement as Thane happily destroyed everything he'd suggested.

Then they parted. Driving his own car, Thane took the motorway route into Glasgow and reached the Western Infirmary exactly on visiting time.

Staff Nurse Blair was hovering around the door when he walked into Phil Moss's ward. She nodded but didn't speak and stayed watching until he arrived at Moss's bed. Then she turned away quickly and went into a side room.

'Thanks for coming,' said Moss. Though his face was still pale, he showed signs of further improvement. Propped up on his pillows, smelling of hospital soap, he had managed to get a cigarette burn on his pyjama jacket. 'Nurse Dracula told me you called back.'

'And got curious.' Thane brought over a chair and sat down. 'So what's going on?'

'You're lying here, in boredom alley, and you've nothing else to do but notice things.' Moss lowered his voice. 'Remember I told you about that emergency appendix job, John Gillan?'

'Across the ward –'

'Don't.' Moss made it a low snarl of warning as Thane went to glance round. 'Just listen, will you?'

'Go burst a stitch,' said Thane wearily. 'All right, how is Gillan?'

'Mending.' Moss sucked his teeth. 'Nurse Dracula's law – nobody dies in her ward without permission. Anyway, Gillan had visitors yesterday, just after you left. Then again last night. The first time, Gillan looked worried as hell once they'd gone. The second time – well, the poor basket was in a state. He lay awake most of the night.'

'Meaning you did too, watching him.' Thane sighed. 'You said visitors. What about them?'

'A man and a woman – the woman about thirty, blonde, sandpaper complexion, and nobody's loving wife. Anyway, Gillan isn't married. The man –' Moss pushed himself up on his elbows – 'Colin, how long since you last saw Charlie Grunion?'

'He's still inside,' protested Thane. 'He got seven years.'

'Then he's got a double,' said Moss. 'Maybe he was a good boy and they let him out early. He was here, Colin. And he scared the hell out of Gillan, whatever they talked about.'

Thane sat silent, frowning. Charlie Grunion was what was known in Glasgow as a wee hard man. Small, runtish, he had two skills – his ability to use a knife and a gift when it came to handling explosives. He'd been sentenced to seven years for combining the two, blowing open a bank safe, then stabbing the first of two cops who tried to arrest him. The second cop had clubbed Grunion with a metal bar which 'just happened' to be lying in their patrol car.

'Did Grunion spot you?' he asked.

'Like this?' countered Moss sarcastically. 'No chance – and when I came in I asked the nurses not to broadcast that I was a cop. Anyway, Grunion wasn't a Millside case.'

Which was true. Grunion had been picked up in Central Division. The Millside involvement had been formal evidence about a stolen car he'd used.

'Maybe he just likes spreading a little joy among the sick,' suggested Thane, then made a mock duck as Moss raised a threatening fist. 'All right, he scares Gillan. What have you got on Gillan?'

'He's thirty-two, a truck driver, works in Glasgow, and lives in lodgings.' Moss paused. 'That's all I could get out of Dracula, but maybe you can do better.'

'I'll make noises,' promised Thane, rising. 'If there is anything, you'll hear. But I won't be back in for a couple of days – I've got to go up to Speyside.'

'Now there's a hardship,' jeered Moss, settling back. 'When you talk to that damned woman, watch her – she's the kind who keeps the bedpans in the deep freeze.'

Leaving him, Thane glanced across the ward as he walked away. All he could see in John Gillan's bed was an anonymous, apparently sleeping huddle under the sheets, only the top of the man's head showing. But Moss was right. Anyone who had Charlie Grunion as a visitor invited interest.

69

He slowed as he reached the side room, saw Staff Nurse Blair arranging dressings on a trolley, and went in.

'Mind if I close the door?' he asked as she looked up.

'You'd better.' She nodded, her round face colouring. As the door closed, her fingers tapped in worried style on the edge of the dressings trolley. 'Well, Superintendent?'

'There could be a small problem in your ward,' he said carefully. 'Right now, I need to know a little more about Gillan.'

'I'm sorry.' Staff Nurse Blair shook her head firmly. 'Information about patients is confidential – it could cost me my job.'

Thane nodded sympathetically. 'Think of it as a welfare matter, and I've a bad memory for names.'

She hesitated, biting her lip.

'Patient records for the ward are in that cabinet, top drawer,' she said suddenly, and turned away in a rustle of starch from her uniform. 'It isn't locked. I – I've got to get this trolley finished.'

Thane opened the drawer, flicked his way through the files, found the one marked John Gillan, and scanned it quickly.

The notes were brief but all that he needed. John Gillan, home address 26 Dellus Street, Glasgow, occupation truck driver, employed by Lancer Transport Ltd, Riverhead Quay, had collapsed on the pavement in Ravell Street, about 11 p.m. An emergency telephone call had been made by an anonymous passerby, an ambulance had brought Gillan in, and he'd been operated on as an emergency appendectomy. His next of kin was listed as a brother, Peter Gillan, who lived in Liverpool.

Thane memorized the addresses, put the file back in place, closed the drawer, and kept back a smile at the way Staff Nurse Blair was still fussing with the dressings trolley.

'I'm finished,' he said quietly. She nodded but refused to look round.

He drove straight home from the hospital, left his station wagon in the carport at the side of the house, went in, and found the place empty except for the dog. Remembering guiltily that Wednesday afternoon was when Mary usually did a volunteer stint at an old people's club, Thane made himself a cup of coffee, drank it, then went to the telephone and called Criminal Intelligence at Police Headquarters.

'A safeblower called Charlie Grunion,' he told the duty officer who answered. 'He drew a seven-year stretch – how long has he been out?'

The man asked him to hold on, there was a gap of about a minute, then he came back on the line.

'Grunion was released two months ago, maximum remission. He must have kept his nose clean for a change.' There was a rustle of paper. 'As far as we know, he emigrated to London.'

'He's back,' said Thane flatly. 'Seen around with a woman, blonde, plenty of mileage on the clock. Can you check it out?'

'We can try,' said the duty officer. 'Is he – ah – lining up something?'

'He might be,' said Thane. 'That's why I'm asking.'

Thanking the man, he hung up and thought for a moment. John Gillan's lodgings in Dellus Street and Ravell Street, where he had collapsed, were both in

71

Marine Division territory, though far apart. But the Lancer Transport depot at Riverhead Quay was just over the border into Millside Division. That was one place where he reckoned he could ask a favour.

He used the telephone again, called Millside Division, smiled wryly as the familiar switchboard voice answered, and had his call put through to Chief Inspector Andrews.

'Forget something when you left, sir?' asked his successor with a cautious joviality.

'No.' Thane could guess what Andrews was thinking. Being a new divisional chief was difficult enough without having yesterday's boss coming on the line. 'I've a mild interest in Lancer Transport, at Riverhead Quay – a friendly whisper that someone might be lining them up as a target.'

'When?' asked Andrews sharply.

'I said might,' soothed Thane. 'I've nothing firm. But if someone could take a look at them without making any fuss about it –'

'We'll do that,' agreed Andrews briskly. 'I'll let you know.'

'There's no rush,' said Thane, and replaced the receiver. He'd kept his promise to Moss, a few wheels were in motion, and for the moment he could put the matter out of his mind.

Sergeant Francey Dunbar arrived twenty minutes later driving the same dirty blue Ford. He stopped the car outside the house, leaned on the horn for two short blasts, then stayed in it, waiting.

By then, Thane was ready. He'd packed his overnight bag and had changed into an old tweed suit which had leather patches at the elbows. Where they were heading, it would blend in better than a city business suit. A note he'd scribbled for Mary was propped against the TV screen, the one place where it was bound to be seen. He picked up the bag, said goodbye to the dog, and went out.

'Hell, it's a country squire,' said Francey Dunbar with mock awe, leaning out of the half-opened driver's door. Dunbar himself was wearing a red wool shirt, blue serge trousers, a windbreaker jacket, and what looked like a pair of government surplus paratrooper boots. 'Going for an audition, sir?'

'The patches are for real,' said Thane frostily. 'What about you, Francey? Planning to climb a mountain or something?'

'Survival gear,' said Dunbar defensively. 'It gets cold up there.'

Thane tossed his overnight bag into the rear, then thumbed Dunbar over towards the passenger seat. His sergeant looked slightly hurt but obeyed and, getting in, Thane started the Ford and set it moving.

'Nice around here,' said Dunbar, glancing at the houses. 'You've done all right.'

'It's called a mortgage,' said Thane dryly.

'I've got a bedsitter near Queen's Park.' Dunbar settled back, grinned, and nodded ahead. 'Look at that pair of grubby young villains.'

Thane looked at the two tousled children in schoolclothes who were using a schoolbag as a football, kicking it along the gutter.

'They're mine,' he said sadly, honking the horn and waving to Tommy and Kate as the car went past them.

'Any more word about our dead man?'

73

'The fingerprints don't match with local records, there's still no word back from London.' Dunbar unwrapped a stick of gum with delicate, loving care. 'Superintendent Maxwell said to tell you the bullet that killed him was from a nine mil. Luger – the same gun as before. He thought you'd be interested.'

'Remind me to thank him,' said Thane gravely. 'That makes my day.'

'Not exactly a woman's gun, is it?' suggested Dunbar.

'Depends on the woman,' countered Thane.

Dunbar blinked, nodded, and fell silent.

It was a good day, they had a fast car, and the A9 north was a main trunk artery. But even so, the 130-mile distance to Speyside meant they had four hours of driving ahead – the A9 was that kind of road. It still owed as much to cattle tracks, to mountain passes, and to the old clan raiding routes as it did to modern surveying. Sheer geography made that hard to change.

There was motorway to Stirling, where the autumn sun glinted on the austere, towering battlements of the historic castle which had once been the heartbeat of a nation. But after that, as farming land gave way to wooded hills, the A9 artery narrowed and began to clog with traffic. Beyond the town of Perth it became a snaking, twisting, unpredictable ribbon of tarmac with occasional race-track straights of newer construction, and all the time the countryside gradually changed, hardening.

Birnam village was the seventy-mile mark. It still had some of the original trees that had worried Shakespeare's Macbeth. Further on, the tourist town of Pitlochry was a traffic tangle where the shops sold salmon fishing gear. Then, once through the dark, wooded ravine called the Pass of Killicrankie, the real Highlands began – the first deer fences, the gradual encroachment of rock and purple heather, of moorland and stunted scrub.

The A9 set its own pace and demanded patience. Most of the time, Thane had to submit and slot the Ford into place in the flow of traffic heading north. Slouched down in the passenger seat, eyes half-closed, Francey Dunbar hummed under his breath and didn't seem to care.

Heavy construction work, a new section of road being blasted out of the rock, brought the pace down to a crawl on the long climb over Drumochter Pass, and by then they were driving deep into mountain country. Heather and granite scree reached down to the roadside, signs warned of the permanent danger of falling rock, and some of the bald, flat-topped peaks which rimmed the horizon wore their early snowcaps.

'They're starting,' said Francey Dunbar, pointing ahead.

A silver thread of a stream traced its way down the side of the nearest slope. At its foot, a small cluster of buildings and two tall chimneys marked a whisky distillery which used the mountain water.

It was as good as a signpost. A mile or so on, the road suddenly swooped down into the long green slash of a narrow valley, with the broad, turbulent, salmon-rich River Spey running through its middle.

Speyside meant a better road and faster travel, with more distillery chimneys like punctuation marks every few miles. The villages they passed were filled with tourist cars and earned their living from them and the mountains, with shops that sold plaid rugs and deerskin bags and motels which were bases for summer pony-trekking and winter skiing. Tiring, Thane gave his passenger a thankful nudge at the sight of a sprawl of white concrete not far ahead, beside a dark, hog-back hill.

'Aviemore,' he said with a degree of relief.

It was their turn-off point, a one-time sleepy village that had been developed – traditionalists said raped – into a multi-million-pound tourist complex of package deal hotels and conference facilities. Slowing, Thane took the next road on the right which was signposted for Crossglen. The car's tyres spitting loose gravel, they headed east, towards the mountains again.

Five miles on, the road skirted a small loch. The car rumbled across a metal-framed bridge. In the fading light, they could see a small village on ahead, but their destination was closer. Another minute and they had swung into the car park of the Ironbridge Hotel, a long, modern, chalet-roofed structure set in a waste of broken rock and backed by a long hill covered in straggling scrub pines.

Inside, the girl at the reception desk wore a tartan jacket and skirt uniform. She also used French perfume and treated Francey Dunbar to a particularly lingering smile as they registered.

Their rooms were along a corridor to the left, on the ground floor and adjoining, small but clean and comfortably furnished. Once he was alone, Colin Thane unpacked his travel bag, washed, then went over to the window and considered the view. His room looked out from the back of the hotel towards the scrub pine hill and there were some sturdy, shaggy-coated ponies moving in a small, barren paddock near at hand. Already, with darkness coming down fast, they were little more than shadows in what promised to be a clear, frosty night.

He checked the room thermostat, turned it up a couple of notches, then made his way along to the bar. It was on the other wing of the hotel, winter après-ski in decor, with a large stone hearth for a log fire and mountain murals across the walls.

Francey Dunbar was sitting at the bar counter, which was pinewood like the tables and chairs. He wasn't alone, and the man he was talking to looked up with a dry curiosity as Thane joined them.

'Evening,' said the stranger. 'I'm Angus Russell. Uh – get me another whisky, son.'

The latter instruction was aimed at Francey Dunbar, who blinked. Two whisky glasses were already on the bar counter in front of them, Dunbar's hardly touched, the stranger's almost empty.

'My round.' Thane signalled the barmaid, ordered, then faced the man who was their designated contact.

Angus Russell deserved a second glance. He was a small, stocky man, bald, leathery-skinned, and probably on the wrong side of sixty. What was left of his hair was white, he hadn't shaved for a couple of days, and he wore an old sheepskin waistcoat, toggle-fastened, over a grey wool shirt, khaki climbing breeches, long wool socks, and heavy rubber-soled climbing boots. A small 35 mil. camera was slung round his neck on a metal chain and a blue beret was partly crammed into one of the waistcoat's large pockets.

'You know why we're here?' asked Thane.

77

'Not yet.' Russell grinned, showing an alarming gap in his front teeth. 'But like I told the boy here, who knows whether you'll tell me the truth anyway?'

Francey Dunbar glowered. Thane paid for the drinks as they arrived, Russell emptying his first glass at a gulp while that was happening, then they left the bar counter and moved across to an empty table. It was still early enough for there to be only a few other customers scattered around.

'Now, which is it you want – my professional skill or the local gossip?' asked Russell, sitting back like a small, secretly amused gnome. He winked at Thane. 'Your sergeant would make a good portrait study, one I could sell to a wild-life magazine.'

'You mean you know how to use that camera?' asked Dunbar, goaded into heavy sarcasm.

'You might say that. Weddings and school prize-givings, babies on rugs – it earns me a living.' Russell was unperturbed. 'For preference, I use it on the hills – a stag at sunrise or an eagle in her nest. Yes, it's a handy thing, a camera.' He turned to Thane. 'Well?'

'A man visited Speyside last week.' Thane nodded to Dunbar, who drew out one of the photographs they'd brought north and laid it in front of Russell. 'He's dead now. His name was Carl Pender – we want to know where he went and who he met.'

'Aye.' Russell's small, keen eyes considered the photograph. 'A passport enlargement?'

'Yes,' agreed Thane. 'He was Danish, he spoke good English, and he was driving a green Chrysler Avenger. That's about all we've got.'

'Speyside's a long stretch of road,' said Russell. 'Tourist territory – would you like to guess how many thousand people a week pass through, even at this time of year?' His hand reached out and the photo-graph was scooped up, to vanish inside the sheepskin waistcoat. 'I'll ask a few people.'

Thane frowned. 'The fewer the better. We don't want this advertised.'

'When I say people, I mean friends,' said Russell. 'I'll lie to them anyway – tell them I'm helping a lawyer looking for divorce evidence. That'll make it more interesting for them.' He took a sip from his glass. 'Would your man Pender use his real name?'

'He might, he might not.' Thane watched Russell set down his glass, realizing it was the older man's first taste at it since his opening performance at the bar. First impressions weren't necessarily valid in judging Angus Russell. 'But we reckon he came north to do a deal. That might have been here, in Crossglen.'

Russell raised an eyebrow. 'Then maybe he stayed at this hotel.'

'He didn't,' said Francey Dunbar. 'I checked – fished around it, anyway.'

'I wondered why you chose the Ironbridge,' mur-mured Russell. 'One of the Aviemore hotels would have been a better base, ordinarily. Well, there are other places he might have stayed – or maybe the people he met up here had a spare room.' He fingered the camera chain at his neck. 'You said a deal. What kind of a deal?'

Thane shook his head. 'That's our worry, not yours.'

'Thanks,' said Russell. His leathery face impassive, he sipped at his glass again. 'All right, Pender – what else?'

'How much do you know about the Glendirk dis-tillery?' asked Thane.

'They make a good whisky,' said Russell, showing surprise. 'A lot of folk liken it to the Tamnavulin malt over on the River Livet, and that's a fair compliment.'

'Pender visited the Glendirk place,' interrupted Francey Dunbar.

'So do plenty of people,' sighed Russell. 'Son, they run daily tours for visitors – you get a free dram on the way round, then buy a bottle or two before they let you out again.'

'Even so, tell me about it,' insisted Thane.

'If you've time to waste,' Russell said. 'Glendirk distillery is small, old-established but modernized, and an independent family business. The last owner was a man called Fraser, but he died a few years back. His daughter Margaret inherited; her husband is a Canadian, Robin Garrett, and he runs it now.'

'Do you know him?'

'You could say that.' A wisp of a grin crossed Russell's face. 'I think I called him a sour-faced idiot the last time we met. We were having a small disagreement about something.' He shook his head. 'Garrett's as straight as they come. And he doesn't need to get involved in deals – malt distilleries are producing liquid gold these days, even with the damned taxation.'

'He might still be able to help,' said Thane slowly. 'I'd like to meet him.' He paused, thinking. 'Know anything about a girl called Marion Cooper – blonde, mid-twenties, plain –'

'Drives a blue Austin,' finished Francey Dunbar in a murmur.

'No.' Angus Russell looked at them blankly.

'How about a man called Chester, about the same age, sallow face, long dark hair?' persisted Thane.

80

A momentary, almost startled flicker of doubt crossed Russell's face but after a second or two he shook his head.

'Sorry.' He said it casually. 'Why? Do they matter?'

Before Thane could answer, a warning grunt came from Francey Dunbar. The girl from the reception desk was walking across the bar towards their table.

'Telephone call, Mr Thane,' she said with a smile that ignored him and concentrated on Dunbar. 'I thought I saw you heading in here.'

Thane followed her back to the lobby, where there was a small, glass-walled telephone booth near the reception desk. He went in, closed the door, and lifted the receiver.

'Did I drag you away from a drink?' asked Maggie Fyffe's voice over the line.

'Francey's guarding it.' He glanced through the glass of the booth towards the reception desk. The girl had gone back to reading a newspaper and the small switchboard behind her was unmanned. 'What's your problem?'

'You wanted to know about your dead burglar in the Cooper woman's apartment,' said Maggie Fyffe, as if discussing the price of groceries. 'Fingerprints match with a London-based all-rounder, Morrie Pascall – convictions for armed robbery, breaking and entering, grievous bodily harm. There's a telex from the London Met. About him –'

'Who did he work for?' cut in Thane, his hand tightening on the receiver.

'Nobody steady.' Maggie Fyffe sounded almost apologetic. 'But they make him sound expensive, and his usual spare-time scene was around the Soho clubs.'

'It still helps.' Thane cloaked his disappointment. At least he now knew for sure that the outside interest was real, determined, and anything but amateur. 'Anything else?'

'No, Superintendent. Not unless you're interested in the fact that my feet hurt, that this is the second night this week I've had to work late, and I've missed my favourite TV programme,' she countered. 'Just go back, and enjoy your drink.'

He chuckled, said goodbye, and hung up. Turning, Thane started to open the glass door of the booth, then froze. A group of people were going out of the hotel door and at the same time another figure was coming in – a young man in a blue anorak. It took a moment for his sallow face and long, dark hair to register, a moment when their eyes met across the lobby area.

Spinning round on his heel, the figure went back out into the night as Thane dived from the telephone booth.

The departing group, elderly people, clogged the doorway as Thane reached it. He shoved his way through, saw his quarry sprinting along the side of the hotel building, and set off in pursuit.

The figure ahead reached the end of the building and kept on, plunging out of the pool of light from the hotel into the darkness of the night. Following, his feet pounding over the mixture of coarse soil and broken rock, Thane heard a startled whinnying from somewhere near and knew they were passing the paddock area he'd seen from his window.

He was feeling the pace. But in the faint moonlight the gap between him and the man ahead was beginning to shrink. Thin, knee-high scrub clawing at his legs, Thane kept on – then suddenly his quarry seemed to hesitate, and veered sharply to the right.

Gasping for breath but seeing his chance, Thane changed direction too, angling across the broken ground to cut the man off. A thicker line of scrub loomed in front of him, he smashed through it and then the ground simply seemed to vanish beneath his feet.

He crashed down, tumbling, ending up in a sprawled, cursing heap on the stony bottom of some kind of massive ditch. Dazed, he struggled to haul himself to his feet again – then ducked frantically as a heavy stone about the size of a brick hurtled out of the darkness and smashed into the ground close beside him.

Another equally large stone followed a moment later, then he heard running feet, feet which faded quickly.

Giving up, Thane stood for a moment panting for breath, realizing what had happened as he looked around, then up at the night sky.

He was in some kind of drainage ditch, about six feet deep and almost as wide, but fortunately dry at the bottom. To his left was the open mouth of what, till then, was a piped culvert. That was why the younger man had made his surprising change of course, and Thane had fallen neatly into the trap, intended or not, when he'd tried to cut the angle.

Calling himself a fool, he clawed his way back out the way he'd come in, struggled through the masking line of scrub, took another step forward, then stopped as a totally unexpected and powerful torch-beam shone into his face, almost blinding him.

'Having trouble?' asked a man's voice, cool and sympathetic. The torch-beam came closer, still on his face. 'You look like you need help.'

'I took a tumble. I – I'm all right,' said Thane. He could just make out two people behind the torch-beam. One might be a woman – he couldn't be sure. He put a hand up to shade his eyes. 'Could you lower that thing a bit?'

'Sorry.' The torch-beam lowered a fraction. Then the man behind it said, 'You've dropped something. At your feet – beside you.'

Automatically, Thane glanced down. He heard a rustle of movement, the torch-beam shifted, then a savage blow took him behind the ear and he pitched forward, the world a red haze which became a deep, black pit as he lost consciousness.

The last thing he heard was a woman's laugh.

Chapter Four

Colin Thane came round slowly, with the feeling there was a sledgehammer thumping somewhere inside his skull. Gradually he realized he was on his back and looking up at the night, which puzzled him because he knew he had fallen face down.

Dazed, still confused, he felt something hard digging painfully into his spine. It was a moment or two before he had the sense to shift clear of the corner of rock which was doing the jabbing. Then, as his grip on reality strengthened, he sat up and nursed his aching head between his hands. A lump was gathering behind one ear, but the skin wasn't broken and he sighed, guessing that the torch which had clubbed him must have been rubber-sheathed.

He looked at his wristwatch and the luminous dial showed he could only have been unconscious for a few minutes. But he was alone now, totally alone with only the night wind murmuring through the thin scrub around him. Fumbling for his cigarettes he lit one, then the tiny flame of the lighter showed his wallet and warrant card lying on the ground beside him. The wallet had been opened, both had obviously been examined, and he understood then why he'd been rolled over on his back.

Thane stowed them back in his inside jacket pocket, took a few more draws on his cigarette, then tossed it away and managed to stand up.

Staggering the first few steps but gradually steadying, he began the walk back towards the glowing lights of the Ironbridge Hotel. He had covered more than half the distance when he heard a shout, a small torch flashed, and first Francey Dunbar, then Angus Russell hurried out of the darkness to meet him.

'What the hell happened to you?' demanded Russell, who had the hand-torch and stared at him in its light. 'You look like you had a fight with a train, man.'

'And lost,' said Francey Dunbar soberly. 'Are you okay, sir?'

'No, I'm not,' snarled Thane.

'That's not so bad, then.' Russell's leathery face, not much more than a silhouette in the night, showed something like relief. 'When you didn't come back, we came looking for you –'

'And the girl on the desk said she saw you go bolting out the door for some reason,' completed Francey Dunbar in a puzzled voice. 'What happened?'

'I saw someone I knew.' Thane glared at Russell. 'Twenties, sallow face, long hair – the one I asked you about who calls himself Chester. Maybe you don't know him but he damned well knows his way around here – he tricked me stupid, straight into a drainage ditch.' He paused, drawing a deep breath, intending to go on.

'Then we're blown,' said Francey Dunbar sadly.

Thane nodded, then hesitated. His sergeant's face was a woodenly diplomatic mask, whatever he was thinking. But something like a spasm of agitation had crossed Angus Russell's shadowed features, then had gone again, leaving only an apparently worried concern. Without being certain why, Thane decided against telling the rest of the story.

'We're blown,' he agreed harshly, his eyes still on Russell. 'Sallow face and long hair – and he's here.'

'There's plenty fit that kind of description, whatever they call themselves,' said Russell in an uneasy voice. 'We're only a handful of miles from Aviemore, and it's full of drifters.' He laid a hand on Thane's arm. 'Do you still want to meet Robin Garrett tonight?'

Thane nodded. 'Front door style – we're not pretending any more.'

'Let me arrange it,' said Russell slowly. 'I'll phone him – it might help. Then I'll talk to a few people, like I promised. Give me a couple of hours and I'll call you.'

Thane agreed, shivered a little in the wind, and was glad as they began to walk towards the hotel again. Russell left them as they reached the car park. He climbed into the driving seat of an old Land Rover and moments later, headlamps blazing, it growled away towards the road.

'Exit, ruffled,' said Francey Dunbar, turning to Thane as the Land Rover's lights disappeared. 'I was taught that boss cops aren't supposed to get the rough end of a deal – that's why they have sergeants. I'll buy you a drink to square things.'

'Fine, once I get cleaned up,' said Thane wryly as they began to walk towards the hotel again.

'I'll – uh – come along with you,' added Dunbar as they reached the doorway. 'Just in case you want to tell me what really happened out there.' He eyed

Thane calmly. 'Either there's more, or it was a bloody big ditch.'

'Both,' said Thane, and led the way in.

Nobody paid any attention to them as they crossed the lobby. Once in his room, Thane stuck his head under the cold water tap for a spell and felt better for it. He used a towel cautiously, then checked the rest of the damage. His tweed jacket was torn in a couple of places and one shoulder was slightly grazed. One trouser knee also had a tear and the skin beneath was split and still bleeding. He washed the blood away, slapped on an adhesive dressing from the little first-aid kit which was in his travel bag, and decided the suit was still just presentable.

'So,' said Francey Dunbar hopefully, 'what happened?'

'I got clobbered,' said Thane, slipping his jacket on again. His head still throbbed and the knee felt stiff, but otherwise he felt back to normal again. 'That was after the ditch.'

Dunbar listened to the rest and gave a soft, sympathetic whistle. 'This man and woman – sounds like we're really blown all round. Think they were maybe following Chester or whatever his name is, and wanted to know why you butted in?'

'Yes,' agreed Thane bitterly. 'Which makes it look like everybody's here.'

'Them and us,' mused Dunbar. His young, not quite handsome face unusually grave, he removed a pellet of gum from his mouth and used finger and thumb to flick it neatly across the room into a waste basket. 'Funny thing, though –' He let it die there.

'Go on, Sergeant Dunbar,' said Thane. 'What's funny?'

'Angus Russell.' Dunbar frowned. 'He's our contact, the Squad has used him before, but –'

'Well?'

Dunbar shrugged. 'After you left to take that phone call he tried damned hard to pump me for more detail about what was going on and why we'd come here. He got edgy about it.'

'With you, that's possible.' Thane sucked his lips. 'What did you tell him?'

'That I was just a low, common detective sergeant,' said Dunbar, 'that I just did what I was told.'

'We'll keep it that way,' said Thane. 'And that phone call, Francey – it was Maggie Fyffe. Our dead man was a London pro, the expensive kind.'

Dunbar sighed, nodded, and got to his feet.

'That drink,' he said. 'Mine is going to be a large one.'

They had their drink in the bar, which was becoming busier. Most of the customers were obvious tourists, and from the talk around most of them had spent the day either hill-walking or more expensively at the Aviemore Centre's less energetic attractions.

The noise chased Thane and Dunbar through to the restaurant. From the menu, they found they'd landed on a traditional Scottish night – and Thane's heart sank at the thought. Some of the courses on offer looked like a gastronomic minefield.

They picked plain and carefully, settled for cock-a-leekie soup, avoided the hazards of salmon fritters and something called howtowdie, and chose brown trout fried in oatmeal.

When the soup came, it was thick enough to walk on. As they finished and their plates were removed by a tartan-uniformed waitress, Francey Dunbar drew an abstract pattern on the tablecloth with the tip of a fork.

'I was thinking,' he said. 'Suppose the couple who thumped you are staying here, in the Ironbridge?'

'They might be.' Thane's eyes roamed around the restaurant, which was filling fast. The hotel had sixty bedrooms and was obviously heavily booked, and all he had to go on were two vague silhouettes, a man's voice and a woman's laugh. 'What do you want to do? Line everybody against a wall?'

Francey Dunbar grimaced, but didn't stop. 'Then how did they get a lead to Crossglen, how did they know?'

Thane shrugged, and the arrival of the trout ended that discussion though the puzzle remained in his own mind.

After the trout, they just managed to sample the hotel's Caledonian Cream – a sweet made from cottage cheese, marmalade, sugar, lemon juice, and a generous melding of malt whisky.

Thane was balancing out the possibility of stretching their expense sheet to a liqueur to wrap things up when the waitress came over to say one of them was wanted on the telephone. He sent Francey Dunbar, who was only gone a couple of minutes.

'Angus Russell,' he said, sinking back into his chair. 'The distillery boss is expecting us at his home in twenty minutes.' He paused and frowned. 'After that, Russell wants to see us at his place – he says it could be important.'

Thane nodded, gave up the liqueur idea, and started thinking about his meeting with Robin Garrett.

It would have to be played low-key and carefully and the Glendirk link was still an unknown quantity ... even though it was just about all he had.

Robin Garrett's home was a big stone house set back from a hill road half a mile out of Crossglen village. Thane and Dunbar got there on time, drove up a crunching gravel driveway, and parked near the front porch, where a light was burning. The upper floor of the house was in darkness but chinks of light showed behind the curtains of the ground-floor windows and they could hear music coming from a radio as they left the car and climbed the few steps to the front door.

Thane rang the doorbell, heard the music switched off, and glanced back at the view while they waited. The lights of the village twinkled down below and a heavier concentration of light marked the Glendirk distillery. Then, as a backcloth, the mountains rose in stark, black silhouette. Whoever had built the house had chosen the site well.

He turned as he heard the door open. The man who stood framed in the light was medium height, in his late forties, greying, but still handsome and well-built. He wore a white roll-neck sweater and tan slacks, and his face held a slightly puzzled welcome.

'Superintendent Thane?' A soft, Canadian accent in his voice, he took the answer for granted and beckoned them in. 'I'm Robin Garrett. Look, I'm not sure what this is all about, but Angus Russell seemed to think it mattered, so –'

Garrett closed the door once they'd entered, nodded as Thane introduced Francey Dunbar, then led the way down a wood-panelled hallway into a large, expensively furnished lounge. A woman in a lime wool dress was curled up on a couch beside a crackling log fire. She was a brunette, with a trim figure, delicate features, and cool green eyes, and she stayed as she was, no particular welcome in her manner.

'My wife, Margaret,' introduced Garrett. 'Uh – sit down, Superintendent. You too, Sergeant.'

They settled in a couple of chairs while Garrett joined his wife. Margaret Garrett looked a few years younger than her husband. There was a drink on a small table at her side, a large solitaire diamond ring glinted in the firelight as she reached out a hand for the glass, and she had a silver chain round her waist as a belt.

'I won't ask if it's a social call,' she said lazily, her eyes on Thane. 'And knowing my husband, he's waiting till you tell him what this is all about.'

Robin Garrett flushed. 'It saves them telling it twice –' he began.

'That's what I mean.' She shrugged and sipped her drink, while Garrett stayed silent.

'Do you know a man called Carl Pender?' asked Thane bluntly.

Husband and wife exchanged a glance, then shook their heads.

'Should we?' asked Margaret Garrett, giving a puzzled frown.

'Francey.' Thane waited while Dunbar rose and showed them each in turn one of the passport photograph enlargements. 'That's Pender, Mrs Garrett. He's dead – killed in a hit-and-run accident near Glasgow Airport. But we believe he was at the Glendirk distillery last week.'

92

'Supposing he was, would it matter?' asked Robin Garrett. He shaped a slightly incredulous grin. 'I mean, what's the connection?'

'None on its own,' said Thane. 'But anything Pender did interests us right now. Pender was a Dane – do you have any Danish business connections, Mr Garrett?'

'Not directly.' Garrett rubbed a hand along his chin. 'In export terms, Glendirk whisky hasn't much of a European penetration, except maybe in West Germany. We've concentrated more on the North American markets –'

'And we don't know any Danes,' said Margaret Garrett impatiently, cutting him short. She leaned forward a little. 'Suppose you let me ask a couple of questions, Superintendent. I know most of the local police by sight. Where do you come from? And what makes this man Pender so important?'

Thane shrugged, ready for both.

'We came north today, from Glasgow. We want to back-track on everything Pender did before he died – because the Danish police had a thick file on him. They reckon that anywhere he went, it wasn't for pleasure. He had to be setting up some kind of criminal operation.'

'And it wouldn't die with him,' murmured Francey Dunbar, breaking his silence. He grinned with a touch of deliberate insolence as Margaret Garrett treated him to raised eyebrows, then took the arranged cue he'd been fed. 'We're Scottish Crime Squad, Mrs Garrett. If someone steals your jewellery, we don't want to know. But Carl Pender was big-time. He didn't come to Speyside without a damned good reason.'

'You make him sound interesting,' said Margaret Garrett with a touch of sarcasm. 'I'd almost have liked to meet him.'

Robin Garrett shook his head slowly, uncertainly. 'He could have been at the distillery, I suppose. We let people visit as – well, a sales gimmick.'

Thane nodded. 'Angus Russell mentioned it.'

'He would,' said Margaret Garrett tartly. She finished her drink and curled into a new position on the couch, then grimaced. 'I'm sorry, but that little man isn't one of my favourite people.'

'He's all right,' said Garrett defensively. 'You've just got to take him as he comes.'

'Your opinion, not mine,' said his wife, then ignored him. 'Superintendent, we've told you we don't know Pender. Is there anything else you want to ask?'

'Just one thing,' answered Thane. 'Who actually shows visitors around at Glendirk?'

Robin Garrett blinked. 'Well, we've a hostess, Joan Harton – it's a part-time job.' He glanced at his watch. 'She was showing a bus-load around tonight, people from a car sales convention in Aviemore. She should still be at the distillery.'

'Then take them to see her and get it over with,' suggested Margaret Garrett. For a moment, her green eyes seemed to mock her husband. 'I certainly don't mind, you know that.'

'Yes.' Garrett's mouth tightened. He got to his feet deliberately and moistened his lips. 'Yes, you're right. If you want to come now, Superintendent '

Thane nodded. He and Dunbar got to their feet, and Margaret Garrett gave them a smile which held its own built-in amusement.

'I hope you find out what you want,' she said. 'But

I doubt it – whatever Robin hired our Miss Harton for, it wasn't her brains.'

They left her there. Outside the house, Garrett declined their offer of a lift and got into his own car, a green Volvo station wagon.

'That's a bitch, and she doesn't care who knows it,' said Francey Dunbar as he set their Ford trundling after the station wagon on the short drive down the hill towards the village and the distillery. 'If I was Garrett, I know what I'd do with her.'

'Her daddy owned the distillery,' reminded Thane. 'Garrett maybe knew what he was buying.'

He felt a moment's sympathy for the soft-spoken Canadian, then shrugged in the darkness. It was none of their business. 'Stay with the car this time, Francey – at least till Garrett's out of sight. Then take a look around on your own.'

'Looking for what?' asked Dunbar.

'If I knew that, I'd tell you,' said Thane acidly. 'Just do it, and don't get caught. And give me one of those photographs of Pender – we still might get lucky.'

They reached Crossglen village a couple of minutes later. The single main street was almost deserted as the two cars purred through, then the Glendirk distillery showed ahead. The Volvo's brake lights glowed and, slowing, the car turned right to stop at a gate in a high security fence. As the Ford pulled in behind it a man emerged from a small gatehouse, opened the gate, and waved them through

Glancing back, Thane saw the gate being closed again as the two cars moved slowly through a clutter of outbuildings and storage sheds. Then they entered a large, brightly lit courtyard and stopped. Getting out of his car, Garrett came towards them and raised a mildly surprised eyebrow when only Thane got out to join him.

'What about your sergeant?' he asked.

'He's happy where he is,' said Thane vaguely, looking around, his nostrils catching the first sweet-sour scent of malted barley, the main distillery block, modern and glass-fronted, immediately in front of him with two gleaming giant copper stills towering almost to its roof. But there were no other vehicles in the courtyard. He glanced inquiringly at Garrett. 'Maybe we're too late.'

'Joan will be around,' said Garrett. 'Getting rid of a bus party is one thing, tidying up after them is another.'

He led the way towards an old stone building on their right, slate-roofed and with whitewashed walls. Somewhere near, Thane heard the low purr of a forced-draught furnace, and, coming through it, a steady murmur of water.

'This was the original distillery – old Great-grandfather Fraser built it over a hundred years ago,' said Garrett. 'Now it's office and reception space, with a cooper's shop for repairing barrels at the rear.' He gestured in the direction of the newer building. 'We opened the new plant not long before Margaret's father died – it was one hell of a battle to persuade him we needed it. But we doubled production and future profits, so like a true Scot he died reasonably happy.'

'What about today?' asked Thane, as they reached a heavy oak door studded with ironwork.

'What about it?' Garrett reacted defensively, a frown creasing his face.

'Production, profits.' Thane could see two men in overalls working behind the glass of the main building. He nodded towards them. 'Things look fairly healthy if you need a night shift.'

Garrett relaxed and gave him an almost pitying look. 'A lot of distillery work is a constant process – you can't switch things off and go home. We've always got a skeleton night shift and security.' He gave a slight chuckle, opening the door. 'Yes, we've certainly got security.'

They went in, and Thane found himself standing in a long, warm room which had rough, dark rafters overhead, stags' heads and crossed swords mounted along its stone walls, and a waxed pinewood floor.

'Our visitor reception area,' said Garrett unnecessarily. The room held a scatter of chairs and small tables, several publicity displays for Glendirk whisky, and a small bar, which held a single whisky cask with a tap and measure. 'I'll go and find Joan. Take a look around if you want.'

Garrett left him, vanishing through the door at the rear, and Thane gave the nearest of the publicity displays a casual inspection. It showed the Glendirk layout in model form, beginning with the two basic ingredients essential to any malt whisky – mountain water direct from a stream beside the distillery and malted barley, kilned over a traditional peat fire then germinated in the long malting shed across the courtyard.

Any Scot knew the rest practically from birth, at least in basic terms. The malted barley and mountain water became a mash, which, once yeast was added, began a three-day fermentation process into alcohol, an alcohol which had to be distilled and distilled again before the final spirit flowed out as a colourless stream as clear as the mountain water which began it all. The amber colour came later, absorbed from the wood of the casks in which the malt whisky would lie for the long years while it matured for marketing.

He smiled, studying the model in more detail. Robin Garrett didn't waste much in the process. The grist and waste mash were salvaged as high protein cattle food and the residual heat from the oil-fired stills was pumped off to heat the whole distillery area.

The process was simple enough. It came down to precise craftsman skill, an art. Then his lips pursed in a silent whistle of appreciation at the printed tag which lay beside the display. At current values, before tax, the Customs-controlled storage warehouses at Glendirk held maturing malt whisky which would eventually be worth twelve million pounds.

Four times the street value of the amphetamine operation which had brought Carl Pender north –

'Find it interesting?' Robin Garrett's voice was unexpected. 'I sketched the original.'

He turned. Garrett was coming down the room towards him, a tall, good-looking woman by his side. She was carrying a large, leather-bound book under one arm.

'It's well done,' said Thane, as they reached him.

'Clean and straightforward, the whole layout,' said Garrett, his eyes on the model, his thoughts obviously on the life-size operation. 'Though I had plenty of opposition whenever it was a new idea.' He shrugged and came back to the present and the woman at his side. 'Sorry, Joan, this is Superintendent Thane. Like I told you, he wants to check on last week's visitors, one in particular.'

Joan Harton gave Thane a friendly nod. She was in her mid-thirties with short, raven-black hair, carried herself confidently, and was smartly dressed in a rust-brown two-piece suit.

'That's why I brought the visitors' book,' she said in a dry voice which lacked the local Highland accent. She took the book from under one arm, and explained, 'Anyone who does the tour is asked to sign, Superintendent. Name and address, then if we want we can do an advertising mail-drop later.'

'What about this man?' Thane produced Pender's photograph and showed it to her. 'Do you remember him?'

'Last week?' Joan Harton frowned at the photograph for a moment, then slowly shook her head. 'Sorry, no. We had maybe a couple of hundred people through last week, and – well, you don't worry too much about faces.'

'Then try the name Carl Pender,' suggested Thane. As Joan Harton nodded and opened the visitors' book, he added, 'If he did sign, he might have given a Danish address.'

The woman began checking pages. Shuffling his feet, Garrett frowned politely.

'From what you hinted, would he use his own name?' he asked pointedly. 'Joan's right about the rest. We advertise visiting times in the local hotels and people just come along. It's like herding a flock of sheep.'

'Does anyone else here get involved with them?' asked Thane.

'I hide from them.' Garrett rubbed his chin, then

brightened. 'But there's always Shug MacLean, our foreman. Joan, he's working late tonight, isn't he?'

'In the still room, or he was.' She turned another page, her finger ran down a final section of names, then she closed the book and looked up. 'Sorry, Superintendent. No luck.' She glanced at Garrett. 'Why not take him along to see Shug?'

'That would settle it,' agreed Garrett. 'At least as far as we're concerned. Thanks, Joan, you get finished off and go home.'

Joan Harton nodded, smiled at Thane, put the book back under her arm, and left them. As she disappeared into a small office at the back of the reception area, Robin Garrett touched Thane's arm.

They set off. Thane had a moment's worry in case they went out into the courtyard again, thinking of Francey Dunbar, who should be prowling by now. But he relaxed as Garrett used a side corridor from the reception area which brought them out into the bright, purring world of the still room, dominated by the giant copper stills.

There was no one in sight. Garrett led the way again and they passed the network of gleaming pipes and glass-fronted spirit safes – the latter with their compulsory double locks, one key held by the distillery, the other by the local Customs staff so that H.M. Government couldn't be deprived of revenue. Customs control was tight in the whisky industry. Even the amount of liquor likely to be lost by evaporation depended on Customs-approved calculations rather than what actually happened.

There was a quieter area behind the main still room. Catwalks and galleries ran beside giant wooden tubs where liquid mash lay fermenting. Garrett looked round, then pointed and gave a call. A burly man in overalls came towards them along one of the cat-walks, cleaning his hands on a rag.

'Just checkin' that number two washback, Mr Garrett,' said Shug MacLean hoarsely as he arrived. A heavy-faced, unshaven man, shirt-sleeves rolled up, tattoo marks visible on both arms, he gave Thane a cursory glance, then added in the same hoarse voice, 'No problems.'

'Fine,' said Garrett and thumbed at Thane. 'Shug, the police are visiting us, looking for help.'

'And it'll only take a minute.' Thane produced Carl Pender's photograph again. 'Ever seen this man?'

'Don't know him,' grunted MacLean after a quick frown at the photograph. 'Why?'

'How about last week's visitors?' persisted Thane. 'Take another look.'

'Don't need to,' said MacLean. 'Like I said, I don't know him, never seen him. What's he done anyway? Picked up too many parking tickets?'

'Something like that,' said Thane.

Then he stopped, startled, as a sudden, loud, banshee-like burst of cackling noise came from some-where outside. The burly foreman spun round, swore, then set off back along the catwalk at a lumbering run. On the way, he snatched a heavy spanner from a work-bench.

'Someone prowling,' said Garrett, looking startled. 'We'd better go with him.'

They both hurried after MacLean, followed him down a flight of iron steps at the far end of the cat-walk while the banshee cackling continued outside, then had to wait for a moment while the foreman slapped down a heavy light control switch, then

101

unbolted a small door. MacLean threw the door open and charged out.

They followed him into a floodlit patch of open ground, with the dark shape of a long warehouse building not much more than a stone's throw away. The cackling reached a new crescendo – and Thane winced as he saw the rest. Francey Dunbar was out in the middle, a flock of angry, wing-flapping geese honking and surging around him.

'Shug –' Garrett grabbed MacLean by the arm, stopping him. 'It's all right. He's a cop, I know him.'

'Then what the hell's he doin'?' demanded MacLean angrily, lowering the spanner. He scowled at Thane. 'Any more of your comedians out there?'

'Just that one,' said Thane stonily, while Dunbar beat a retreat towards them, pursued by two very large, irate geese.

The geese backed off as they saw the other humans. Once the four men were back inside, MacLean slammed the door shut, bolted it again, and shut the light control.

'Sorry,' said Dunbar sheepishly. 'I – uh – just thought I'd take a look around.'

'Well, you met our security squad.' Garrett's eyes glinted with amusement and something else which was hard to read. 'Just plain, ordinary geese, Sergeant. Plenty of distilleries use them – they kick up one hell of a useful din if anything disturbs them.'

'And they bite.' Dunbar rubbed his left leg and winced. 'Like I said, I'm sorry.'

Shug MacLean grunted, his disgust plain. Then, turning, he walked away.

'We've caused enough chaos for one night,' said

Thane. He smiled wryly. 'Thanks for your help, Mr Garrett. We'll find our own way out.'

Garrett frowned uncertainly. 'You haven't sampled the product. That's a tradition '

'Another time,' promised Thane.

Garrett was still frowning as they left him and headed back along the catwalk.

They were in the Ford and driving out of the distillery before Francey Dunbar uttered another word. He sat chewing an edge of his straggling moustache, eyed Thane sideways, then carefully cleared his throat.

'Never did like bird life much,' he ventured.

'They seemed to feel the same way.' Thane waited while the distillery gate was swung open. Then, as Dunbar drove out and they turned on to the road, heading for Crossglen village, he sighed. 'Well, do I have to drag it out of you? What else did you trip over?'

'Something that compensates.' Dunbar kept his eyes on the dark road ahead. 'They've a staff car park and – uh – there's a blue Austin in it.' The glow of the instrument lights showed his mouth shape a grin. 'I sort of leaned against the boot lock with a piece of wire and it opened. There's a smell like something died inside that luggage space –'

'The same smell?' Thane sat bolt upright and grabbed his arm as Dunbar nodded. 'You're sure?'

His sergeant nodded. 'That amphetamine pong, sir. Positive, and a hell of a lot stronger.'

Thane swore happily to himself. 'You locked the boot again?'

'And got the registration number,' said Dunbar. 'Uh – does that square those damned geese?'

'Puts you ahead,' said Thane. He lit a cigarette and sat silent, thinking, while the car reached the start of Crossglen village and began travelling along the main street. Suddenly, curtly, he ordered, 'Slow down, Francey. We're going back.'

Obediently Dunbar slowed, took the car round in a U turn, then let it coast to a halt.

'Marion Cooper,' said Thane quietly. 'Long blonde hair, plain, isn't seen around much. Right?'

Dunbar nodded cautiously.

'Joan Harton has short dark hair, dresses well, looks good. She's only at the distillery part-time.' Thane used his cigarette like a pointer in the night. 'Try it.'

Dunbar whistled his understanding. 'A wig –'

'A blonde wig, and who knows what the hell a woman looks like when she takes her make-up off,' said Thane soberly. 'The one we've got here is going home soon. Let's see if she does anything else first.'

A few minutes later they were waiting, lights and engine switched off, the car drawn half off the road on a grass verge, with the distillery gates a bright pool of light ahead. Time passed slowly and Thane was almost ready to believe they'd missed out when the distillery gates were opened.

The car which emerged was a blue Austin, and it swung left and came down the road towards them. They sank down in their seats as it passed, but Thane still had a clear view of the driver – and it was Joan Harton.

'Now?' asked Francey Dunbar.

Thane nodded, then stopped him just as quickly. A second car's lights had blinked to life on the road just beyond the distillery. In another moment it also passed them, a grey-coloured Fiat with one man aboard. He was in no hurry, but his intention was plain. They weren't the only people intent on following the distillery hostess.

'What the hell now?' demanded Dunbar, surprised.

'Follow my leader,' Thane told him. 'But hang back – keep it as loose as you can.'

Dunbar nodded, started the Ford, and they swung round again. By then, the Fiat's tail lights were mere small red dots ahead and all they saw of the blue Austin in the lead was an occasional sweep of headlights as it took a bend.

They drove that way for about five miles, through Crossglen village, then past the Ironbridge Hotel on the winding, tree- and rock-fringed road towards Aviemore. Humming quietly, his face a serious mask, Francey Dunbar showed he'd plenty of experience as he juggled with distance, speed, and the need to keep that vital minimum of visual contact – then, at last, the Fiat's pace slowed and its brake lights flared briefly.

'Damn,' said Francey Dunbar conversationally, slowing in turn, killing their lights at the same time. He kept the Ford crawling forward in the darkness, Thane glancing behind and thankful the road was otherwise empty.

Then, having almost stopped, the Fiat accelerated away. Dunbar let it go for a moment, then switched on the Ford's lights and followed again. Seconds later they saw the reason for the strange manoeuvre as they passed a small group of cottages by the roadside, each with a handkerchief-sized garden at the front.

The doors of the small garage at the side of one cottage were open. The blue Austin had been driven

105

in and Joan Harton was just on the point of closing the garage again.

Which left the Fiat, still on ahead, freed of shadowing and travelling faster. They had passed a signpost which said two miles to Aviemore when, unexpectedly, the red tail lights vanished. Francey Dunbar gave a groan, then changed it to a sigh of relief as Thane pointed to the left.

The Fiat had turned off the road and was threading along a roughly surfaced track between trees. Beyond the trees was a scatter of lights. They understood why a moment later when they reached the start of the track and saw a motel sign.

They followed in, the Ford bumping and swaying along the track, and as they emerged on the far side of the trees Francey Dunbar let the car trickle to a halt, off the track, almost hidden by a bank of thick gorse.

The motel was ahead, a scatter of wooden chalets around a modest central office and restaurant block, and the Fiat had stopped beside one of the chalets on the left. The Fiat's lights went out, the driver emerged, crossed to the chalet, went in, and lights showed at its windows a moment later.

'My turn,' said Thane. 'Just stay awake.'

He left the car to an uncomplimentary mutter from Dunbar. A couple of minutes was enough to let him cut across the coarse grassland which surrounded the motel; he skirted two chalets which were occupied, then reached the one he wanted.

The curtains hadn't been drawn. Working his way round, he looked in at two empty bedrooms, then edged to the next window and drew back, pressing against the wall, after his first glance.

A man was moving around a small living room. He

106

was tall, he was broad-shouldered, heavy-faced, and had his jacket off and his collar and tie loosened. Thane chanced another glance, in time to see the stranger open a can of beer and take a first swallow.

Built like a traditional cop – the description came into his mind almost without Thane realizing it. Then that linked back, to the phoney sergeant who had turned up near the airport after Pender's death.

He started to retreat from the chalet, then stopped short and instead crouched back in its shelter again as another car came purring out of the trees, passed the motel office, and headed towards the chalet. The car, a dark blue Jaguar, pulled in beside the Fiat, stopped, engine and lights were switched off, and a man and woman got out. The man was medium height and wore a top-coat, the woman was in slacks and a hip-length suede jacket, and they went straight to the chalet door.

It opened as they reached it. He heard a murmur of voices, then the woman laughed, and it was a laugh he remembered only too well. As the couple went in, he saw she was a brunette and that the man with her had thin features and dark, shoulder-length hair.

The door closed. Inside the chalet, the curtains were drawn. He listened for a moment, heard nothing more beyond an occasional murmur, took a last long look at the registration plates on both cars, then made his way back to where the Ford was concealed.

'Gave me my worries, seeing that Jaguar come in,' said Francey Dunbar as soon as Thane was back aboard. 'Know any of them, sir?'

'No, but I can put labels on them.' Thane laid his head back against the seat, fitting things together for a moment.

Most of it still came down to guesswork, to circumstance. But the three in the chalet, whoever they were, had already come as far along Carl Pender's trail as he had managed. Perhaps, for all he knew, even further, and narcotics worth three million pounds on the streets made an impressive stake for them by any standards. Three – and they'd started out as four. They would be more careful now, careful and doubly dangerous.

And he was realist enough to know that if they required extra muscle, then a telephone call and a few hours' wait were all that would be required to bring it north to Speyside.

'Sir –' Francey Dunbar's voice broke into his thoughts. 'We were supposed to go and see Angus Russell. It's getting late.'

'I know.' Thane frowned in the darkness, trying to sort out his priorities. If he had still had his Millside divisional team – he shrugged, and put that firmly out of his mind. 'Get your notebook out.'

Dunbar wrote while he dictated the car registration numbers and the scanty descriptions of their occupants. When that was finished, Thane waited until he had tucked the notebook away.

'I'll talk to Russell on my own.' Thane made it clear there was no discussion involved. 'You'll have to break the glad news to the local cops in Aviemore that we're up here, though they may have heard from their Headquarters. I want one of their men to visit the motel on some kind of excuse and find out anything he can about these three.'

Dunbar sighed but nodded. 'And the rest of it?'

'Feed the car registration numbers and everything else by phone to the S.C.S. night shift in Glasgow.

Tell them that as soon as they've sorted out a computer check on the cars they'll save time if they get straight on to London, to the same people who knew about Morrie Pascall.'

'It'll still take time,' warned Dunbar.

'They've got till morning. And you'd better stay with it.' Thane motioned him out of the driving seat. 'Now swap over, and tell me how I find Russell's place.'

Ten minutes later he dropped a disgruntled Francey Dunbar at the little police station in old Aviemore village, then drove off again, heading through the modern, over-shadowing sprawl of the Aviemore Centre.

It was coming up for midnight and as he followed the one-way road system the whole playground development of hotels and bars, restaurants and amusement areas was still a bright bustle of noise and life. Thane drove through it carefully, the road system busy with cars shuttling passengers in everything from jeans to full evening dress, a cinema emptying, a pipe band marching up and down for some reason in a central square.

Yet beyond the Centre boundaries was the start of an empty wilderness. Rock and bogland, mountain and ravine, scrub pine and hungry wildlife – he passed the silhouette of an artificial ski-slope, skirted a children's playground, which had Father Christmas in residence all year round, then, following Francey Dunbar's directions, took a turning off to the left.

In a few hundred yards, he was back in the wilderness world. A narrow track which couldn't be called any kind of road climbed rapidly. He turned left again at a junction, the headlights reflecting back brought animal eyes from the verge, and soon he saw a cottage ahead.

There was a light at its window. He parked outside, used the heavy iron knocker on the cottage door, and it was opened by Angus Russell.

'You're late on the road,' said Russell, letting him in. 'I was beginning to wonder.'

The door closed and Thane followed the stocky, white-haired photographer through into a front room which was obviously part office, part living quarters. A gas heater blasted out warmth beside an old desk covered in photographs and order forms, more photographs were pinned around the walls, and the only carpeting on the floor was an old deerskin rug.

'Sit down, man.' Russell waved him into the nearer of two shabby, broken-down armchairs. 'You'll have a dram –' he made it a statement, not a question, producing a bottle and two chipped glasses as he spoke – 'though I won't guarantee it'll match the Glendirk stuff.'

'We passed that up,' said Thane.

'Did you?' The man's gnome-like face registered surprise, then he poured two drinks, handed one to Thane, and took a quick swallow from his own. 'And – uh – how did you make out with Robin Garrett?'

'No luck,' said Thane deliberately.

'Aye.' Russell settled in the other chair and sat silent for a moment, watching Thane sipping at his glass, the gas heater purring in the background. 'Well, I spoke to some friends, like I said I would. You were right about one thing, Superintendent. Your man Pender passed this way.'

'Passed?' Thane raised an eyebrow at the word.

'That's right,' said Russell smugly. 'Stayed at the Mail Coach Hotel one night last week then headed north, came back and stayed another night, two days later.'

'What makes you so sure he went north?' asked Thane, his face expressionless.

'He bought an extra map at the filling station beside the Mail Coach and checked the routes north of Inverness with the pump attendant,' said Russell, and took another long swallow from his glass. 'Looks like you've been wasting your time here, doesn't it?'

'Then what about the character I chased tonight, the one who landed me in that damned ditch?' asked Thane.

'I – maybe you were wrong.' Russell hesitated and forced a weak grin. 'Maybe it was just someone who looked like your man, eh?' He took another gulp at his drink, watching Thane closely. 'If someone like you started chasing me, I'd run. I'm built that way.'

'I'll think about it,' said Thane. He had made up his mind before he spoke. Though he wasn't totally sure why, he no longer completely trusted the photographer – whatever might have happened in previous S.C.S. dealings. He let himself relax back in the shabby armchair and glanced around. 'Live on your own here?'

'For a long time,' answered Russell. 'I've got a wife somewhere, if she's still alive. Haven't seen her for close on twenty years.' He rose, topped up his glass, and shrugged when Thane shook his head at a similar

111

offer. 'While you're here, take a look at how I earn a living.'

For the next few minutes he showed Thane a variety of photographs from the prints scattered around. They were good, particularly the scenics, and as he described them Russell's manner thawed and became relaxed again.

At last, when Thane rose to go, Angus Russell bade him an almost fond farewell.

'I'll maybe not see you again,' he said at the cottage door. 'No real reason, eh?'

'Maybe, maybe not,' said Thane in a totally neutral voice.

Russell stayed at the cottage door to watch him drive off.

By the time Colin Thane got back to the Ironbridge Hotel he felt tired.

Once in his room, he sat on the edge of the bed and smoked a cigarette, thinking again.

What Russell had told him about Pender's apparent stay was probably true – Russell wasn't fool enough to lie about it. But the hire car's mileage ruled out any expedition much further north and the road map story was a professional's typical cover action.

He grinned for a moment, wondering how Francey Dunbar was getting on with the local cops. Then he thought of Russell again.

Russell wanted them out, away from his part of Speyside.

But that wasn't going to happen. The amphetamine operation was tied in, somehow or other, with Glendirk distillery, and while Joan Harton headed the list there, maybe Robin Garrett himself might not be far behind.

He undressed slowly, yawned as he got into bed and switched off the light, and was asleep within minutes.

Chapter Five

It was bright and sunny the next morning, the blue sky a perfect backcloth for the rich green of the hills and the grey rock streaked with snow which waited higher up.

Colin Thane woke early to the sounds of a pony-trekking expedition setting off from the paddock behind the hotel. He washed, shaved, ran a comb through his thick, dark hair, considered himself in the mirror, and decided in a moment's self-indulgence that for forty-two he'd worn reasonably well. He had almost finished dressing when the bedroom door was unceremoniously shoved open and Francey Dunbar padded in.

'Morning,' said Dunbar wearily. He went over to the window, looked out, and yawned. 'Dawn's early light.' He glanced round at Thane and added accusingly, 'I didn't get back till five this morning. Nearly came in then, to tell you.'

'Be glad you didn't.' Thane slipped into his jacket and checked the pockets for the basics – money and cigarettes. 'How did you make out?'

'Pretty good, sir.' Dunbar's lean young face split in another monumental yawn. 'The local cops were friendly, once they decided I was for real. Fed me coffee and fried egg sandwiches.'

'I'm not interested in the cuisine,' said Thane. He lit his first cigarette of the day, which meant another day when he wouldn't have stopped smoking. 'Get on with it.'

'Records say they've nothing on any Joan Harton, distillery hostess or anything else, but we've got three beauties in that motel.' Dunbar leaned back against the window-sill, his laconic voice suddenly business-like. 'The Jaguar's registered owner is Frank Benodet, London address. He runs an antique business, but he's on the London Met. Drug Squad books as a narcotics wholesaler with plenty of European connec-tions – major league, not top of the tree, but big.' Pausing, Dunbar let a slight grin crinkle the edges of his moustache. 'The Met. boys say the woman has to be Miriam Vassa, his common-law wife – she's his regular Girl Friday.'

'And the big fellow?'

'Could be a character called Coshy Jackton. He's trouble too,' said Dunbar. 'He was a cop for a spell in the Midlands, then got jailed for off-duty robberies. Now he's Benodet's odd-job man and minder.'

'Nice people.' For Thane, the sunlight outside his hotel window suddenly seemed to dull and the peaks took on a new harshness. He sighed. It was still pretty much as he'd expected, down to a man who knew the routine when it came to posing as a policeman. He took a slow, meditative draw on the cigarette, which no longer tasted good. 'What else?'

Dunbar shrugged. 'The other car they've got is a local hire job – they must have picked it up when they got here, which was yesterday. The Aviemore sergeant sent one of his men along to the motel, and they're keeping an eye on the place – it helps that the manager owes them a few favours. Benodet, the woman, and Jackton arrived about midday yesterday, no advance reservation. They paid cash and that's all the manager knows – or cares.'

'It fits.' Thane knew he didn't have to spell it out to Dunbar. Benodet had come north, with some kind of lead to the deal Carl Pender was interested in. Even after Pender's death, it had been enough of a lead to take him to 'Marion Cooper's' apartment in Glasgow. That, in turn, had cost him one of his team killed, but he must have waited, played it cool, trailed the blue Austin which had brought her north overnight. Then been able to fit enough pieces together to know he was close to his goal, the amphetamine factory.

'So.' Dunbar stifled a yawn, pushed away from the window-sill, and took a brief, disgusted glance at himself in the mirror. 'Life's rough at the bottom. Uh – how did you make out with Angus Russell?'

'He wants rid of us.' Thane told him the rest.

'It smells.' Dunbar looked perplexed. 'What the hell is he playing at?'

'Maybe we'll have to find out,' said Thane.

'He has a son.' Dunbar frowned. He saw Thane's surprise and nodded. 'Sean Russell – he's a skiing instructor, works the local hotel trade around here in the winter. The Aviemore cops know him – seems he and his father had a big fall-out years ago, and parted company. But the worst trouble he's been in is an occasional driving offence.' Then, guessing what was on Thane's mind, he shook his head. 'They don't know we've been using father.'

'Keep it that way for now.' Thane stubbed out his

116

half-smoked cigarette and grimaced. 'Don't make waves, Francey, not till we know who they'll hit in the face. How about the Harton woman?'

'Lives alone, arrived in the district a few months ago, went straight to work for Garrett as distillery hostess.' Dunbar chuckled. 'Seems that raised an eyebrow or two, but if they've anything going they don't wave it around in public.'

Which left Shug MacLean, and all Dunbar had managed to obtain in the way of gossip was that the distillery foreman was a local man, married with two teenage children, had worked in the distillery for several years, and had acquired the tattoo marks on his arms from a spell in the Regular Army.

'Everybody knows something about everybody in this part of the world,' mused Thane as Dunbar finished. 'That's why nobody ever used to bother locking a door.'

'They do now,' reminded Dunbar. 'It's called civilization.'

They ate breakfast in the hotel, left shortly afterwards, and drove into the Aviemore Centre at about 10 a.m. The sun was still shining, the day was pleasantly mild, and the Centre's playground areas were busy with tourist trade. That meant fat women plugging around on hired bicycles, teenagers queuing to get into the main swimming pool or the indoor ice-rink, and bus parties forming up to set off on sightseeing tours.

The Mail Coach Hotel, where Carl Pender had stayed, was close to the heart of it all. They left the Ford in the nearest car park and went first to the hotel and then to the filling station beside it. A few questions in each place established that Angus Russell's story was based on fact as far as it went.

'Where now?' asked Dunbar, as they left the filling station. His eyes followed a couple of girls in overtight jeans who were passing by, and he sighed a little. 'Look at that – and there's a lot of it about.'

'I'd noticed,' said Thane dryly. He drew a mild satisfaction from deciding he'd spotted the girls a full five seconds before his sergeant. He pointed in the opposite direction, towards a sports goods shop which had window posters advertising that it was a booking agency. 'Save your energy. You're going to be an eager skiing enthusiast who wants to know what his favourite instructor does when there isn't enough snow around.'

'Sean Russell?' Dunbar looked mildly surprised, then nodded. 'That might make sense.'

'Thank you,' said Thane sardonically, and led the way.

The sports store window had a seasonal display of climbing, fishing and camping equipment. But, once inside, where the atmosphere smelled of leather and canvas, they found the stock on view covered year-round sporting activity. While Dunbar went over to the counter to begin a cheerful conversation with a middle-aged male assistant, Thane moved around with a casual interest which was partly soured by the price tags.

Then, suddenly, he came to a halt. He had reached the skiing section. The racked skis, the heavy boots and bright protective clothing were arranged around a central display advertising skiing lessons. In the middle was a photograph of two grinning skiers with, in bold lettering underneath, 'Two of our resident ski instructors, Sean Russell and Pete Stanson.'

Russell was fair-haired, stockily built like his father, and had an arm round the other man's shoulder. Stanson was dark-haired, sallow-skinned – and the man Thane had first seen posing as a reporter near Glasgow Airport, the same man he'd chased unsuccessfully the night before. Thane was still staring at the placard when Dunbar came back to join him.

'Sean Russell's around,' said Dunbar briskly. 'He's helping out at a construction job beside the ski slopes at the East Coirre chair lift. Lives somewhere up there too, in an old trailer caravan and –' His voice died away. 'What's wrong?'

'The reason Angus Russell wants rid of us.' Thane nodded at the photograph. 'There's his son. The one with him is an old friend of mine. Except he called himself Chester.'

'The character you chased last night –' Dunbar, for once, seemed lost for words.

'Ask what they know about him,' ordered Thane. 'I'll be outside, counting up how many more mistakes we've made.'

Dunbar nodded and headed back towards the counter. Leaving the shop, Thane stood with his back to the window and watched the passing tourists, hardly seeing them. His face was grim. Angus Russell had been their safe contact – perhaps he was, in any other situation but this one. But Russell must have guessed that the man Thane wanted was his son's friend. If Sean Russell knew by now –

'Good morning, Superintendent,' said a cool voice, catching him unawares. 'Missing the city?'

He blinked. Margaret Garrett, neat in a white

cashmere sweater and suede skirt, a fur jacket worn loose across her shoulders, stood a few feet away from him. Her eyes were hidden behind large, dark sunglasses and her expression was one of amused tolerance, as if she'd discovered a small dog to pat.

'Daydreaming.' Thane gestured vaguely. 'It happens when you get tired chasing your tail.'

'Meaning your elusive Mr Pender from Denmark?' She paused and grimaced. 'Wrong word. As you told us, he's not elusive, he's dead. You're still trying?'

'Plodding on,' said Thane. He looked around. 'On your own, Mrs Garrett?'

'Yes.' A sarcastic note entered her voice. 'My beloved husband and I don't practise any particular brand of togetherness, Superintendent. That's just how things are – you may have noticed that last night.' She shrugged. 'If you want to talk to him, he's probably at the distillery – that's where he spends most of his time except at weekends. Then he takes himself off into the hills, tramping around and pretending he's some kind of overgrown Boy Scout.'

'You don't approve?' asked Thane.

'I don't give a damn,' she said frankly. 'Any more than I give a damn who keeps his bed-roll warm when he's out there.' She gave a small, humourless laugh. 'Don't look so surprised, Superintendent. There are faults on both sides, and I'm a practical person.'

'I've got nothing to do with marriage guidance,' said Thane. 'But I may have to talk to your husband again – tonight, at home, would do.'

'Suit yourself,' she said, tightening the fur jacket around her shoulders. 'I won't be there – I'm going away for a few days.'

'A holiday?'

'A break – some personal business, and visiting my son. He's a management trainee in Edinburgh.'

This time Thane showed his surprise. 'I didn't realize –'

'His name is Keith, and he'll be twenty-one next birthday.' Her manner softened as she spoke. 'Keith Ornway, his father died in a climbing accident. I married Robin five years after that.' Suddenly she glanced at her wristwatch, a tiny insert in a thick gold bracelet. 'I'll have to go, or I'll be late for a hairdressing appointment.'

'When do you leave for Edinburgh?' asked Thane.

'This afternoon – I'm driving down.' Margaret Garrett gave him a frankly calculating smile. 'It's a pity, Superintendent, but that's life.'

She went away, a slim, confident figure, and moments later Francey Dunbar came over from the direction of the sports shop.

'I didn't want to break up anything,' said Dunbar with a lopsided grin. 'What the hell did she want?'

'Just a brief chat with the peasantry,' Thane told him absently. Margaret Garrett had surprised him in more ways than one, and she'd also given him a few things to think about. But for the moment they would have to wait. 'What about Pete Stanson?'

'I didn't get a lot,' admitted Dunbar, hands deep in his pockets. 'Stanson hasn't been around much since the end of the skiing season. The character I talked to in there thinks Stanson is working in Glasgow, but he did say that Stanson and Sean Russell are close friends. In fact, Russell originally brought him here and got him his skiing job.'

'It helps to know,' mused Thane.

'Yes.' Dunbar hesitated, then glanced sideways at Thane. 'Look, sir, you're the boss. But I think we're getting tangled up in a helluva lot of loose ends –'

'Do you?' Curtly Thane cut him short. 'That's my worry, Sergeant, not yours.'

He saw Dunbar flush and regretted having said it. But he didn't feel in a mood for making apologetic noises.

They went back to the car. He told Dunbar to drive to the village police station, then sat back silent, almost angry at himself, while the car purred along the road.

He knew what was wrong. He was missing Phil Moss. He could have discussed and argued with Moss and been confident that Moss's acid criticism and complaints would have been mere wrappings round some firmly logical suggestions. But though he had already developed a liking for the young, brashly aggressive sergeant sitting beside him it still hadn't developed into any kind of working partnership, not yet, anyway.

Except that Dunbar had been right. Thane sighed to himself, seeing the small police station building not far ahead. So far, they had been collecting loose ends, some major, some important. What he needed now was to shape them into some kind of a pattern before they became an unmanageable tangle.

They reached the police station, turned off the road into the small parking area at the rear of the building, and as the car slowed he heard Francey Dunbar give a sudden, surprised grunt.

'We've got company.' Dunbar nodded towards a small, travel-stained green Mini-Cooper saloon which was lying empty. He stopped the Ford beside

122

it, took another look, and nodded. 'That's one of the Squad pool.'

'Reinforcements,' said Thane dryly.

Dunbar grinned. Thane thought he caught something like relief in his sergeant's eyes.

They left the car and went into the police station. A middle-aged, grey-haired sergeant with a police long-service medal ribbon on his tunic was the only person in the outer office. His name was Henderson, he had already met Dunbar, and he greeted Thane in a relaxed way which meant he was near enough pension age to have stopped worrying about high-ranking visitors.

'I've got two of your people through the back,' he told Thane in a soft Highland accent. 'They got here about twenty minutes ago and I told them you'd be along soon enough.'

'Backing a hunch, Sergeant?' Thane raised a quizzical eyebrow.

'Aye. Anyway, I thought keeping them safe here was better than letting them wander out and get lost,' said Henderson.

Thane grinned. 'What's the latest you've heard from the motel?'

'The folk you're interested in?' Henderson frowned. 'Benodet and the other man went out for a spell in one of the cars before breakfast. They were gone about half an hour, then they came back with what looked like newspapers and groceries and joined the woman again.'

'They haven't moved since?'

'No.' Henderson shook his head. 'I'll hear if they do.' He hesitated, then added, 'What this is all about stays your business, sir. Except that if you do need any help –'

'I will, probably soon.' Thane nodded his thanks.

Followed by Dunbar, he went through to a back room where two people got to their feet as he entered. One was a girl, a tall slim redhead in blue denim slacks and a thick wool sweater. Her companion was a man in his late thirties, balding, stockily built, and wearing a tweed suit which looked even older than Thane's.

Dunbar handled the introductions. The girl's name was Sandra Craig, a detective constable who had graduated to the Scottish Crime Squad from a Glasgow support group team. Joe Felix was also a detective constable, from the Squad's surveillance and technical section, and the girl let him do the talking.

'The commander thought you might need some extra bodies, sir,' said Felix with an unassuming grin. 'I picked up Sandra and a few things you might need. We left at 6 a.m. but – uh –' he sneaked a sideways glance at the girl – 'we had a compulsory breakfast halt.'

'I got hungry,' she said defensively.

'She always gets hungry,' said Dunbar.

'Right now, Francey feels the same way about sleep,' said Thane, saw Dunbar twist a slight grin, and felt relieved. He turned to Felix. 'Can you handle a long-range surveillance with not much cover?'

'Day and night,' said Felix confidently. 'I packed one of the infra-red kits.' He lifted a small briefcase, opened it, and glanced up at Thane. 'The commander said he reckoned you and Francey might want these; we've got our own.'

124

Two well-oiled Webley .38 automatics and a bundle of spare magazine clips came out of the briefcase. Thane took his share and watched grimly as Dunbar did the same. In a handful of years the old image of the British cop as someone who treated firearms as a last resort had faded, eroded away by the sheer growing volume of cases where the opposition came armed and prepared to use their weapons at minimum provocation. So, when guns might be needed they were issued – or carried. To an extent that plenty of retired detectives still alive would have found almost unbelievable.

'Just remember, we're not on any hunting trip,' he said quietly. 'Francey, bring them up to date – all we've got. I'll be back.'

Leaving them, he went through to where Sergeant Henderson was scowling over a batch of printed forms, asked for a telephone, and was taken through to another small room where most of the space was occupied by a stacked heap of mountain rescue gear. The phone was half-hidden under a coil of rope on a small table.

Tactfully Henderson left and closed the door. Lifting the telephone, Thane dialled the Scottish Crime Squad number in Glasgow, then waited while the line clicked and buzzed, his eyes on a poster on the wall which was an illustrated guide to local game laws.

When he got through to the Squad number, it was answered by Maggie Fyffe's assistant. Commander Hart was out, but Tom Maxwell was available and he came on the line a moment later.

'We've sent you some back-up,' said Maxwell cheerfully.

'They've arrived, and I can use them.' Thane left it

at that. 'Tom, I need someone on your end to do some burrowing. Mostly, I'd like to know the financial health of the Glendirk company – it looks good on the surface but the hard cash situation might be different.'

'Different the way that would make sense out of the other operation?' He paused. 'Maggie Fyffe's a good mole – I'll start her working. And I'll give you some free advice, Colin. The London Met. have been on again about your Frank Benodet – don't take chances with him. He's a hard man, the Vassa woman matches him, and the London boys reckon that if it is Coshy Jackton who's with them then you're up against really heavy muscle.'

'So far, they're just sniffing around.' Thane's eyes strayed to the poster again. A snarling wildcat glared at him from one illustration. 'Tom, I'm almost more interested in your contact, Angus Russell.'

'Russell?' A chuckle of disbelief reached him. 'He's an odd character but he hasn't let me down yet. The first time I used him, he practically led me by the hand to a bank raid team.'

'This time he has a son,' said Thane grimly. 'So father is trying to tell us to go away – and I'm beginning to think I know why.'

'Hell and damnation.' Maxwell's voice came low and unhappily over the line. 'His son – Russell told me about him once. The kid got himself thrown out of a university course and they had a hell of a row about it.'

'You wouldn't remember why he was thrown out, or what he was studying?' asked Thane.

'No, but he was studying in Glasgow. I can check.'

'Add another name, his friend Pete Stanson, same age,' said Thane. 'Stanson was our phoney journalist.'

126

'You wouldn't like to stick a knife in me while you're at it?' suggested Maxwell. 'All right. Anything more that's unpleasant and nasty?'

'Not right now,' said Thane.

'Then before you hang up, do me one favour,' begged Maxwell. 'Exactly what has Phil Moss stirred up at that damned hospital he's in?'

'He asked me to check out a couple of things for him,' admitted Thane cautiously. 'Why?'

'Chief Inspector Andrews, your successor at Millside, that's why,' said Maxwell, obviously glad to be off the defensive. 'He came on to me babbling about some trucking company, then about some character who's a patient beside Moss –'

'So?'

'Hell, I don't know,' complained Maxwell. 'Ask Moss, ask Andrews, but don't ask me. But Andrews reckons he's on to something. Says to say thanks.'

'Give him my blessing,' said Thane. 'Tell him I didn't know when I was lucky.'

He hung up and took another look at the wildlife poster, wondering what the average Glasgow cop would make of it. Then he went back out to Sergeant Henderson.

'Any word from the motel?'

Henderson looked up from his paperwork and shook his head. Nodding his thanks, Thane went through to the other room where Francey Dunbar had just finished his briefing session with the two new arrivals.

'You both know the score?' asked Thane.

Felix and the girl nodded.

'Right.' He perched himself on the edge of a desk, letting his legs swing, his grey eyes serious. 'Then

127

remember this – our first priority remains to find the place where this drug is being processed. All we've got so far stays flimsy until we've located it and the processed amphetamine.' He glanced at Francey. 'I'm not renowned for patience but we've got to go warily till then – we can't risk blowing everything because one of us suddenly feels bloody-minded.'

Dunbar shaped a slight, appreciative grin.

'You're hoping someone will lead us to it?' asked Sandra Craig.

Thane nodded.

She frowned. 'Won't this man Benodet have the same idea?'

'Maybe. But he's likely to be more direct in his approach.'

Later, bitterly, Colin Thane was going to remember what he'd said. But for the moment he was primarily concerned with the basics of the operation. He explained quickly how the local police would maintain a watch on the motel. He checked that, as far as possible, Felix and the girl had the descriptions of the main people involved at the Glendirk end. The two S.C.S. cars could stay in radio contact, Felix had brought a couple of hand-held walkie-talkie sets north with him, and as a team they could either operate on their own private channel or link in with the local police wavelength.

'You take Joan Harton, the distillery hostess,' he told Felix. 'Check she's at her home, then watch the place. Radio me if anything starts happening, but stay put.'

Felix nodded. 'How close can I get?'

'You'll have to be off the road. Field glasses and a clump of dry heather.' He turned to Sandra Craig.

'You've got the distillery – Felix can drop you there first, and you'll have a walkie-talkie. Pick your own cover and keep in it.'

'Dry heather.' She grimaced. 'Well, it makes a change from back alleys and beer cans.'

'So enjoy it,' he suggested. 'Francey and I are going to look at a ski-lift. But we'll be near enough if anything does happen.'

The little Mini-Cooper, Felix and the girl aboard, left the police station first. Thane and Dunbar followed in the Ford a few minutes later after a brief word with Sergeant Henderson.

It was about midday, still bright and sunny, but a gathering breeze was ruffling the trees. Thane did the driving, Francey Dunbar keeping himself busy for a few minutes checking out the car's radio channels, and by the time he had finished that they had left the tourist sector around Aviemore and were heading east again.

There were on a narrow but well-surfaced secondary road which climbed gradually at first, skirting a loch where the water was a clear ice-blue and passing a camp site where the canvas of brightly coloured tents had begun to quiver in the gusting wind. Beyond that, they plunged into thick young woodland, the Queen's Forest, the road still winding, Aviemore now shrunk to postage-stamp size far below and the only other traffic an occasional tourist car or a labouring truck.

A deer sprang across the road in front of them as they rounded one corner, and vanished immediately into the trees. Further on, a couple of laden hikers trudged manfully along the verge. A dead hare lay squashed on the tarmac, a cluster of greedy black crows too busy feasting on it to bother moving as the Ford growled past.

Then, suddenly, the tree-line was left behind. On ahead, the road climbed and wound through gorse and rock, punctuated by foaming mountain streams – and above everything towered the cloud-wisped shoulders of the Cairngorm Mountain and its surrounding peaks.

They saw the first chair-lift and ski-tow lines a moment later; small, pylon-supported cableways strung in several directions across the mountainside. In winter, the Cairngorm was the largest skiing area in Britain. But though the snow had melted back to an occasional white pocket among the gorse and rock, some of the cableways were still moving, their chairs and T-bars carrying a few adventurous springtime visitors on sightseeing trips.

A signpost directed them along a side road towards the East Coire ski-lift site, and in another couple of minutes they pulled into a roughly surfaced car parking area. On ahead, a small base camp of huts marked the start point of the new ski-lift and part of the cableway was working, carrying material up to where construction was still going on.

They were about to leave the car when the radio came to life, a just readable voice calling through the heavy crackle of static. Swearing mildly, Dunbar answered. It was Felix.

'Thought you'd better know.' Even through the static, he sounded almost apologetic. 'The local cops at the motel say Benodet's man Jackton has just left in his car. It looks like he's coming my way, towards Joan Harton's place.'

Thane took the microphone from Dunbar. 'What I told you stands, Felix. Just watch – and make sure Sandra is awake at the distillery.'

Felix acknowledged cheerfully and Thane tossed the microphone back to Dunbar.

'You'd better stay,' he decided and shook his head at Dunbar's mutter of protest. 'It could mean nothing, but I'm not taking chances.'

He left the long-faced young sergeant unwrapping a stick of gum, stepped out of the car into a chill, gusting wind, and walked across the parking area towards a group of workmen who were unloading a truck. Edging his way round stacked bags of cement and a tangle of steel girders, he waited for a couple of minutes while the foreman, a tubby, energetic man in overalls, a padded windbreaker jacket and a bright yellow safety helmet, finished giving orders to some of his squad. Then, as the man turned away towards one of the huts, Thane stopped him.

'It's a fair-sized job,' he said conversationally, nodding towards the half-constructed ski-tow. 'A day like this should please you.'

'When we get one.' The foreman eyed him suspiciously. 'Got some business here, mister? We don't allow visitors – we've enough problems without some outsider falling down a hole or getting hurt.'

'I'm just trying to find a lad who works up here,' said Thane soothingly. 'Is Sean Russell around?'

The foreman grunted. 'Are you a friend of his?'

'No, but I thought I'd look him up,' said Thane. 'I know his father.'

'Old Angus?' The foreman visibly relaxed, shifted round a little so his back was to the wind, and grinned. 'We've had him and his camera up a few times. But you're out of luck. Sean's a casual with us – sometimes he's with us, sometimes he isn't. He hasn't been around for a few days.' He paused and shrugged. 'In fact, I expected him to show up this morning, but he didn't.'

Thane grimaced. Behind the foreman, another load of materials had started swaying up the cableway, to be suspended within seconds over a deep, black gully in the mountainside.

'Any idea where he lives?' asked Thane. 'Someone said there's an old caravan –'

'That's right.' The foreman beckoned and led him across the site to a point where the view was panoramic across the forestry plantations down below. 'Straight back down the road, and watch for a white marker stone once you're into the trees. Take a track to the left just past it, and you'll reach an old ruin of a cottage – the caravan's another three hundred yards or so on.'

'I'll try it.' Thane nodded. Then, looking down at the trees, he added casually, 'It must be pretty lonely for him, down there on his own.'

'He shares with a mate.' The foreman shrugged. 'They've got motor cycles and ride them like maniacs.' He treated Thane to a wink. 'Plenty of girls around Aviemore, and I reckon these two make the most of it.'

'Envy gets you nowhere,' said Thane sadly. He thanked the man, and returned to the car, glad to get back into its shelter and escape from the chill, penetrating wind. Closing the door, he shook his head at Dunbar.

132

'Not here, but I know about the caravan.' Then he nodded at the radio. 'Any more word?'

'Yes, sir.' Dunbar's eyes held a glint. 'Something's happening – Felix was on again. Benodet's man turned up at Joan Harton's house, handed in something, and drove straight off again – that was just after you left. I've had Felix on again since. The Harton woman took her car out of the garage straightaway and drove off like a rocket towards the distillery.'

'Contact, or some kind of ultimatum.' Thane whistled tunelessly through his teeth for a moment, his fingertips tapping the steering wheel. 'Sandra will pick her up. Keep listening – we're going caravan-hunting.'

He started the Ford, swung it round in a tight turn, and they bounced back across the parking area to the road. From there, he took off downhill in a way that pressed Dunbar back against his seat at each tyre-squealing bend. Without being certain why, Thane had a feeling time was beginning to matter.

They had just reached the trees when the radio came to life again. This time it was Sandra Craig's voice, cool and precise, cutting through the crackle from the speaker.

'Joan Harton has arrived at the distillery,' she reported dispassionately, as soon as Francey Dunbar acknowledged. 'She drove straight in – I've lost sight of the car for now. Continuing watch.'

She had hardly finished when Felix came back on, equally briefly, acting as a link again for the county men. Jackton had returned to the motel and was back with his two companions in their chalet.

'Mission accomplished,' said Dunbar.

'Or end of round one,' suggested Thane. He saw the question in Dunbar's eyes and shook his head. 'I want to know more about the form before I start any real betting.'

The white marker stone appeared ahead and the track was just beyond it, as they'd been told. The car turned in, bumping and swaying along a rough, badly potholed surface with the trees pressing close on either side. It was like driving through a dark green tunnel, their speed cut back to a crawl and the engine note little more than a murmur.

Suddenly, a small clearing with an old, roofless cottage showed ahead. Thane steered the car off the track, and they lurched in behind the shelter of the tumbledown walls.

Sandra Craig called them on the radio again as they halted. This time her voice wasn't quite as cool as before.

'Something else happening here,' she reported. 'The Harton woman's car has just left the distillery again, but she's not aboard. The driver's a man – that's all I can tell you.'

Francey Dunbar had the microphone. 'Heading where?' he demanded.

'Wait,' she told them. There was only static for a moment, then she was back. 'East – or that's how it looks, so he could be coming your way.'

'Continue watch,' said Dunbar. He laid down the microphone and turned to face Thane. 'She could be right.'

Thane nodded. Whatever kind of message had been delivered from Benodet, it had been important enough to start a flurry of activity. Stonily, he watched Dunbar bring out his pistol and check it, the weight of the Webley in his own jacket pocket an equal reminder against his side.

'Let's go,' he decided as Dunbar tucked the gun away again. 'But get this into your head, Francey – we're not the cavalry, and I don't like heroes. They're usually the idiots who get shot first.'

They left the car, made sure the ruined cottage stonework totally hid it, then set off through the trees keeping parallel with the track.

The construction site foreman had known his distances. At exactly the forecast three hundred yards the trees ended in another felled clearing and they kept back, crouching in cover at the edge. A small stream trickled through the clearing and a dilapidated trailer caravan, most of its paintwork weathered away, sat close to the ribbon of water.

'Over there,' murmured Francey Dunbar, pointing.

A motor cycle lay propped against a tree stump. Wide handlebars, thick treaded tyres, and heavy duty forks showed it was no ordinary road machine but a go-anywhere trail bike. Nodding, Thane took another look at the caravan itself. A window was half-open and a faint trace of smoke came from the rusted chimney-stack which protruded from the roof.

'Someone's at home,' he said softly, then grabbed Dunbar's arm and hauled him down quickly as the younger man started to rise. 'Don't be a damned fool. That's not what we're here for.'

They waited. Ten minutes passed, with still no sign of movement from the caravan. Insects buzzed around them. Dunbar stirred impatiently from time to time, and Thane found himself developing a sudden craving for a cigarette. Then, suddenly, they heard the approaching growl of a car.

Joan Harton's blue Austin lurched into the clearing a moment later and stopped at the same time as the caravan door swung open. Thane swore under his breath as he saw the thin, sallow-faced figure of Pete Stanson come out and got an even bigger surprise when he recognized the driver who emerged from the car.

It was Shug MacLean, the burly Glendirk distillery foreman. An incredulous grunt from Francey Dunbar indicated he had been equally startled.

The two men talked briefly by the caravan, MacLean gesturing with a clenched fist to emphasize what he was saying. Stanson nodded, then hurried back into the caravan while MacLean returned to his car. Seconds passed, then Stanson reappeared wearing a leather jacket and putting on a crash helmet. He went to his motor cycle, started it up, and waited while MacLean swung the blue Austin round. Then, the motor cycle in the lead, the car close behind, they drove off in a cloud of dust and gravel.

'The clan is gathering,' said Francey Dunbar as the sound of the two vehicles faded away among the trees. 'Shug MacLean – one more for the list.' He scowled towards the caravan. 'But what about Sean Russell?'

'He can wait.' Motioning Dunbar to his feet, Thane led the way across the rough, hummocked grass towards the caravan.

The door was locked but the window beside it was still half-open. Thane reached through, his fingertips managed to locate the door handle on the inside, and in another moment they were in the caravan.

It was a grubby, untidy place with two unmade bunk beds, a coke stove for warmth, and a kitchen area which looked as though it hadn't been cleaned for a long time. A blackened coffee pot was simmering on the stove but there was another, stronger odour in the caravan, one which made Thane's nostrils twitch.

'Here we go again,' muttered Dunbar. The insidious, sweet-sour amphetamine smell was mixed with stale cigarette smoke but still unmistakable. He carefully squashed a large black beetle that scurried across the floor at his feet. 'Do we start looking?'

Thane nodded and they began, working to an unspoken routine, each taking one side of the caravan, carefully putting things back in the same kind of disorder in which they were found. At first, the pattern was just what might be expected when two men lived alone in comparative isolation, then, opening a locker under one of the bunks, Dunbar sniffed hard, rummaged for a moment, and called Thane over.

A grubby blue shirt was stained with a dirty yellow chemical residue. Dunbar produced a small plastic bag and scraped a little of the residue into it. Thane made the next discovery in a wardrobe cupboard, a pair of grey trousers with the same spattered staining.

When he checked the pockets of a khaki waterproof jacket, his mouth tightened. One of the pockets held a number of loose shotgun cartridges, and among them, slimmer, obviously overlooked, lay a single round of nine mil. pistol ammunition.

He kept it, and there was nothing else. They left the caravan, closed the door and heard the spring lock work, then went back through the trees to the ruined cottage where the Ford was hidden.

They arrived at the cottage from a slightly different angle and as Thane strode on Francey Dunbar hung back, stopped, then called him.

'What about these?' asked Dunbar, pointing to another clear set of tyre marks in the soft, hummocked ground. 'More visitors?'

'Could be tourists,' suggested Thane, but had doubts almost as he spoke. The marks looked fresh and they tied in with something else which had been forming in his mind.

Dunbar grunted, giving the suggestion scant respect. Eyeing the ground carefully, he shuffled around the tyre marks, then suddenly stooped, peered closely at a small straggle of gorse bush which lay broken and flattened, and looked up at Thane.

'Tourists?' he asked sardonically.

There was dried blood on the gorse and more had seeped into the ground beneath to form a small, blackened crust.

'Sean Russell,' said Thane quietly. He saw Dunbar struggling to understand, and added, 'That's maybe Benodet's move. He has Sean Russell and he has let them know it.'

Dunbar gave a slow whistle of agreement. 'Last night, when we saw Benodet and the woman drive into the motel –'

'They could have come from here.' Thane brushed a hovering insect away from his face, still putting it together in his mind. 'If they trailed Stanson and Joan Harton north, they could have found out about this place. Then, if they came along last night – well, maybe they thought at first it was Stanson they were grabbing.' He shrugged. 'If Stanson came along later and Russell just didn't show up, Stanson wouldn't worry.'

'Probably just wondered who the woman was.' Dunbar gave a dry grin but then his amusement

138

faded. 'If they thought Russell was Stanson, I don't give much for his chances. Not if they reckon Stanson killed their mate down in Glasgow.'

'Just one of the hired help,' corrected Thane. 'Benodet's in the narcotics business. He wants a deal for twenty-plus kilos of amphetamine, Francey. He needs live bait, not a body.'

'I suppose so.' Dunbar sighed and rose to his feet. 'Well, if Russell's alive where the hell have they put him?'

'Somewhere safe till they need him.' Thane prowled around the tyre marks then took a wider circle, knowing what was missing. 'Stanson and Russell both have trail bikes. Where's Russell's machine?'

They found it a few minutes later, hidden further back among the trees, the painted metal partly covered in broken branches. Thane stopped Francey Dunbar as he made to brush them aside.

'No, we'll still let them set the pace,' he said grimly. 'We do nothing about this and say nothing.'

'And what happens if we find Russell dead?' protested Dunbar, combing a hand through his mop of black hair and looking worried.

'Then he won't be exactly able to complain,' said Thane mildly.

'If you say so,' said Dunbar. Then he gave a wry grin and nodded. 'But I'm applying for a nervous breakdown just as soon as we're finished.'

They returned to the car and drove back along the track to the main road. As they reached it, the radio began muttering and Dunbar answered, increasing the volume.

'I've been trying to raise you, Francey,' came the indignant crackle of Sandra Craig's voice over the speaker. 'What the hell are you and our new boy up to?'

Dunbar winced and used the microphone again. 'He's right beside me. I'll ask.'

They heard her groan, then there was silence.

'I'm – uh – sorry, Superintendent,' she said after a moment. 'The situation here is the Harton woman's car came back to the distillery and there was a motor cyclist right behind it. They're both inside, no other movements.'

Thane kept one hand on the steering wheel and took the microphone with the other.

'Understood, Detective Constable Craig,' he said. 'We'll be visiting there shortly.' Then, winking at Dunbar, he added, 'And as the new boy, thank you for your concern. Out.'

He tossed the microphone back and drove on, grinning.

Chapter Six

A few minutes took them to Crossglen village, where the car had to crawl along most of the length of the main street behind a heavy truck and trailer outfit loaded with timber. They got past it just before the Glendirk distillery buildings, turned in, and had to stop at the gate while the gateman telephoned to the office block.

'Relax, think happy,' murmured Thane while Francey Dunbar fidgeted impatiently beside him. 'And we're on a friendly visit – so fasten that damned jacket.'

Dunbar looked down, saw the way the butt of his gun was protruding from the waistband of his slacks, and fastened his windbreaker with a sheepish nod. Thane glanced round, at the low, wooded hill on the far side of the road. Sandra Craig was up there somewhere, maintaining her watch, but maybe she wouldn't have to do that much longer.

The gateman ambled back, gave them a nod, and opened the gate. Driving through, they parked the Ford in the same courtyard they'd used the previous night. The only vehicles in sight were Garrett's green Volvo station wagon and the blue Austin which

141

they'd seen Shug MacLean driving. There was no sign of the trail bike.

Leaving their car, they walked across the courtyard through the sounds and smells of the distillery to the office block and went into the reception area. Joan Harton came forward to greet them, and though her smile held a slightly nervous edge she greeted them cheerfully.

'More problems, Superintendent?' she asked.

'None I'm going to worry you with,' said Thane, noting her lack of make-up, the old wool sweater and tweed skirt she was wearing, and the rumpled state of her short, raven-black hair. Compared with the sleek, smartly dressed woman they'd met before, Joan Harton showed all the signs of someone who'd had reason to come rushing from home. 'But I'd like to see Robin Garrett for a moment.'

'He knows you're here.' She gave Thane and Dunbar another forced smile, glanced over her shoulder, and visibly relaxed as Garrett emerged from an office door at the rear of the reception area accompanied by Shug MacLean. 'It's just one of those days – he had some production details to sort out with Shug.'

The two men came halfway towards them, halted, then the distillery foreman nodded at something Garrett said, turned, and went away. His heavy unshaven face was like a mask and he totally ignored the two detectives. But Garrett came forward confidently, tucking a pen into his jacket pocket, smiling a welcome.

'I thought you'd like to know we've got a firmer lead on Carl Pender,' said Thane straightaway. 'Our information was right – he was around here. To be more exact, he stayed in Aviemore.'

'I see.' Garrett raised an eyebrow. 'I'm sorry, but if he did come to the distillery then –'

'He could have looked in.' Thane didn't let him finish. 'Like you told us, you've plenty of casual sight-seers. Anyway, it looks as though Aviemore was just a stopover before he headed further north.'

'So now you'll have to start looking again.' Garrett made a sympathetic noise, then glanced at Joan Harton. 'Well, we certainly wish you luck, Super-intendent. And – ah – I hope your sergeant didn't lose too much sleep after the way he tangled with our geese last night.'

'They're not my kind of bird life,' agreed Francey Dunbar. 'Fried chicken does me.'

Garrett laughed. 'When are you leaving?'

'Today sometime,' said Thane. He paused, then added, 'I met your wife this morning, in Aviemore. She told me she was going away for a few days – I wouldn't like to think we'd chased her.'

'Margaret?' Robin Garrett gave a slight grimace. 'You didn't worry her, very little does, believe me. But we can't let you go empty-handed, either of you. Joan –'

Joan Harton had moved away while they'd been talking. She came forward again, and handed Thane and Dunbar a wrapped, oblong package each.

'A sample of the product,' explained Garrett. 'But treat it carefully – that's not your off-licence whisky, it's the raw stuff, matured but well over proof strength.' He winked. 'Just don't tell the Customs squad – they wouldn't totally approve.' He glanced at his watch. 'Well, I've things to do, Superintendent. But the best of luck up north.'

They said goodbye, then Thane and Dunbar left. When they reached the car, Thane gestured Dunbar to take the wheel. Once inside, Dunbar frowned at the package in his hands.

'What do we do with these bottles?' he asked cautiously. 'I mean –'

'Token hospitality doesn't rate as bribery,' said Thane. 'What bottles, Sergeant?' He took both packages, put them over on the rear seat, then drew a deep breath. 'Let's go. Nobody is going to move while we're around.'

'But now they think we're going.' Dunbar started the car, then let it idle for a moment, while he chewed on a corner of his straggling moustache. 'What about Pete Stanson? He's somewhere in here –'

'I said let's go,' reminded Thane patiently. He left it at that until the car was through the distillery gates again, then pointed in the direction of Aviemore. 'That way.'

As they started off along the road, he sat silent, thinking not so much of Stanson but of Sean Russell. In Frank Benodet's hands, as he pretty well had to be, the young skiing instructor's chances were slim unless Benodet's bid to force a deal for the waiting fortune in drugs succeeded. But Thane knew there was very little he could do about that. For the moment, he had to keep on and rely on his own reading of what was happening.

'When we get to Aviemore, drop me off at the police station,' he told Dunbar. 'Then I want you to pull in Joe Felix and Sandra, switch them to watching the motel.'

'And leave that bunch back there?' Dunbar kept his eyes on the road but looked startled. 'Why?'

'Benodet gave them some kind of an ultimatum.' Thane paused and winced as a random cyclist weaved for a moment across their path. 'Now he's waiting on an answer, which means a meeting – he's not the kind of fool who would leave a phone number. None of them knows about Felix and the girl, so when Benodet moves they can trail him.'

'Benodet has two cars at that motel,' said Dunbar, accepting the rest.

Thane nodded. 'That's why you'll be there too, as back-up – but only as back-up, remember that. If they all leave, try and get into that motel chalet and take a look around.' He gave Dunbar a slight smile. 'You'll have to play it by ear.'

'And you'll have my guts if I get it wrong,' said Dunbar in resignation, then concentrated on driving.

The sky had become overcast and there was a faint drizzle of rain by the time they reached the police station at Aviemore. Thane got out and went into the building as Dunbar drove off again. Just inside he collided with a familiar, unexpected figure.

'The very man I was looking for,' said Angus Russell heartily. The small, bald photographer wore his usual outfit of sheepskin waistcoat, wool shirt and khaki breeches, and had the inevitable camera slung round his neck. He grinned at Thane, showing the gap in his front teeth. 'I – uh – tried for you at your hotel. Then I looked in here – not that I told any of them I was trying to find you.' He tapped the side of his nose confidentially with a chemically stained finger. 'I know better than that.'

'So now you've found me, why the search?' asked Thane.

'I've nothing new to tell you,' admitted Russell. He

glanced around, as if anxious to make sure no one else was within earshot. 'Have you decided what you're doing?'

'Pulling out,' said Thane, and shrugged. 'What you told us about Pender seems to fit. He must have headed north, so that's where we'll have to try.'

'Aye.' Russell moistened his lips and tried hard not to look pleased. 'What about that fellow you thought you recognized?'

'If he was the same man, he's probably far away by now,' said Thane. 'Anyway, Carl Pender is what really matters.'

'If he knew the trouble he was causing, he'd be laughing in his grave,' said Russell, rubbing a hand across the stubble on his chin. 'Well, do me a favour. When you get back to your S.C.S. pals say hello for me to Superintendent Maxwell – just say it's the same as always, that I'm here, ready to help.'

'He'll appreciate that,' said Thane gravely.

Russell nodded and went out. As the door swung shut on the small, gnomish figure, Thane shook his head and went through to the police station's front counter. The constable on duty there was a stranger, but Sergeant Henderson stuck his head out of a side room and ushered Thane through.

'It's my lunch break,' said Henderson, closing the door firmly once Thane had joined him. He gestured to the packet of sandwiches lying on a table and the opened thermos flask beside them. 'There's plenty if you'd care for a bite.'

'Thanks.' Thane sat down on a spare chair, took a sandwich, and started on it while Henderson poured him some coffee in a mug. 'Angus Russell was leaving as I came in. What did he want?'

146

'Just a gossip, or so he said.' Henderson sat down opposite him and considered Thane thoughtfully. 'Does the wee man interest you, sir?'

'More than he knows,' said Thane.

'Aye.' Henderson nodded wisely. 'We've had the feeling he's helped your people and others like them before.' He chuckled, pleased at Thane's surprise. 'You city folk may think we've got heather growing out of our ears, Superintendent. But we notice things.'

'I learned that lesson a long time ago, Sergeant,' said Thane quietly. He took another bite of sandwich, chewed for a moment, then sipped the coffee. 'The main reason for my interest in Russell is his son.'

'Sir?' Henderson's lined elderly face was puzzled.

'I'm going to need more of your help,' said Thane. 'If that worries you, I'll square it with your divisional bosses.'

Henderson shook his head and grinned. 'I'm a practical man, sir. I've already done that, so tell me what you want.'

'I'll tell you why first, some of it anyway,' said Thane. 'How much coffee is left in that flask?'

'Enough,' said Henderson, and rubbed a hand over his greying hair. 'And if it's a long story, sir – well then, we can get more.'

The flask was empty and Thane had smoked his way through two cigarettes before he finished giving the local sergeant a basic run-down on what had brought him north and what had happened since. At the end, Henderson sat with his eyes almost closed for a moment and muttered something that sounded like a long Gaelic oath. He followed it with a sigh and looked up.

'Six months more, and I'm out on pension,' he said

147

sadly. 'Couldn't they have done the decent thing and waited?' He shook his head in disgust. 'And they drag a damned good malt whisky into all –'

'Sacrilege,' agreed Thane. 'I don't know how some of the pieces fit together. I'm hoping to hear from the Scottish Crime Squad fairly soon and that should help. But what do you know about Garrett and his wife?'

Slowly, lips pursed, Henderson shook his head.

'Very little,' he admitted. 'Just the gossip that they don't get on, with most of the blame thrown her way. Garrett just clings on – not that he has much option.'

'Meaning what?' asked Thane.

'The distillery,' said Henderson patiently. 'His wife owns it – Robin Garrett isn't much better than hired help. Everybody knows that.'

'I didn't,' said Thane softly. 'I should have guessed, but I didn't.'

He had wanted a motive, one that would make a man running a prospering whisky distillery take a dive into the murk and slime of the narcotics world. He had a feeling the elderly sergeant sitting across from him had just supplied it, on a plate.

'So what help do you need, sir?' demanded Henderson after a moment, puzzled by Thane's silence.

'For a start, I want to use this police station as our base.' Thane paused, considering his mental checklist. 'You're already helping at the motel, but I've had to pull out the watch I had on the distillery. Can you take that over?'

'Easy enough,' agreed Henderson, getting to his feet. 'One of my lads can be there in ten minutes, and I'd defy old Satan himself to find him on a hillside – his father was a damned good poacher.'

The forecast was only slightly optimistic. Twelve minutes later the police station's radio crackled to life as the local constable checked in from his observation point. Then, as if on cue, Francey Dunbar called up.

Thane took the microphone in the little radio room. 'All set?' he asked.

'Set and snug, sir,' reported Dunbar cheerfully. 'I've got Joe Felix and Sandra watching the motel and ready to roll. So far, Benodet and the other two haven't moved from their chalet.' He broke off, Thane heard a background murmur of voices, then Dunbar came back again with a chuckle. 'Sandra says she's starving again, but that's our only problem. I'll throw her some raw meat later.'

'When you do, use a long pole,' said Thane dryly. He heard an indignant background protest before Dunbar cut his transmitter switch, and smiled as he laid down his own microphone. He had drawn a good team – not Millside Division style, but in some ways even closer knit – and they were gradually accepting him in.

Time dragged on. In the front office, the routine day continued for the little police station. Two drunks – one local, one visiting – were brought in and locked up after a lunch-time brawl. An English tourist complained that luggage had been stolen from his car, which he'd left unlocked in a parking area at the Aviemore Centre. A teenage girl, spotted hitch-hiking on the A9 road, had been collected because she had spent the night in a lorry driver's cab and had vanished with his wallet before morning. A seven-year-old boy fell into a pond, was rescued almost drowned, and his rescuer had to be rushed to hospital with a coronary attack. Two old ladies complained they'd been locked out of a lavatory and someone handed in a stray dog.

By mid-afternoon the drizzle had gone, the sun had pushed the temperature up several degrees, and Thane had finished another flask of Sergeant Henderson's coffee. Then, just after 3 p.m., the radio came to life.

'Something happening,' reported Francey Dunbar, and paused. 'Yes, Benodet's on the move, sir. Looks like they'll use both cars. Do you want it blow-by-blow?'

'No, wait till it matters,' ordered Thane. 'But tell Felix and the girl to keep it as loose a tag as possible.'

Five minutes later, the soft Highland voice of Henderson's constable watching the distillery crackled in again. Robin Garrett's green Volvo station wagon had just left from there with Garrett driving and Joan Harton in the passenger seat. It was heading in towards Aviemore.

Thane acknowledged, counted the cigarettes he had left, and resigned himself to waiting. Sympathetically, Henderson stayed clear, and the local policemen who came and went followed his example while the police station clock crawled round with an agonizing slowness.

Three thirty came and went, with still no word from the radio. The amount of coffee he'd taken forced Thane to make a trip to the white-tiled, spotlessly clean men's room and as he came out he almost collided with a young constable who had been sent to find him.

The radio was still silent but there was a telephone call for him. He took the call in Henderson's room and it was Maggie Fyffe, her voice brisk and crystal clear over the line from the Scottish Crime Squad office in Glasgow.

'Tom Maxwell said you'd be chewing your finger-nails till you heard from us,' she said, unimpressed. 'He got hauled out on a job – somebody says they're going to blow up a politician but won't give us a name. But I've got some of what you wanted on your amphetamine team.'

'Bless you and damn the politicians,' said Thane fervently. 'Go on, woman.'

'Don't rush me.' He heard her rustle papers for a moment. 'Right. Sean Russell first, and I'll skip what you don't need. Criminal records haven't anything on him, but he got bounced out of the university in his third year. Too much wine, women and song, and he stopped passing examinations.'

'What was he studying?'

'Chemistry,' she said. 'I thought that would interest you. But his friend Pete Stanson is something differ-ent – middle-class background gone wrong, four previous convictions including a couple for serious assault. Special Branch say he went over to Ireland about a year ago ready to wave a gun around for anyone, but both lots decided he was the next best thing to an unreliable psychopath and threw him back again.'

'That fits,' agreed Thane with a sigh. 'Thanks, Maggie. How did you make out with the Glendirk side of it?'

'Now that is even more interesting,' she admitted. 'And it wasn't too difficult either – I got most of it from the Registrar of Companies in Edinburgh. Financially, Glendirk is one really healthy company. There are one or two small fringe shareholders,

151

including a bank, and it looks as if that was done to raise some money a few years back.'

'They had a modernization programme going,' confirmed Thane.

'I feel that way sometimes myself,' she commented dryly. 'But here's what matters. The rest of the set-up is a family trust, the type a regiment of lawyers couldn't break up. Margaret Garrett has full control for her lifetime, then it passes quite specifically to her son by her first marriage, somebody called Keith –'

'Keith Ornway, twenty-one next birthday.'

'A lucky young gentleman,' said Maggie Fyffe enviously. 'His grandfather certainly tied things up so that her second husband couldn't get his hands on the loot.'

'Yes.' Thane felt a moment of something near to sympathy for Robin Garrett. 'You've done a nice job, Maggie.'

'I haven't finished,' she said. 'I borrowed some newspaper library clippings. The Garrett wedding got quite a write-up in the society columns – "tragic widow's happy day", that sort of thing. Like to know what Garrett did for a living before he married a distillery? He was an industrial chemist.'

'Which makes it gift-wrapped,' said Thane. 'Thanks.'

'I do all the real work,' she said complacently. 'And your wife called. I've to tell you your new watch is fixed, whatever that means, and you've to bring her back some Speyside trout.'

'Trout?' asked Thane absently.

'For eating,' she agreed. 'You don't have to catch them – there's at least one trout farm around Aviemore. And I'd like some too. It'll square acting as a messenger girl for your pal Inspector Moss.'

Thane sighed, but had to ask. 'What's he done?'

She chuckled. 'Found himself a payroll truck hijack, set for tomorrow, except now the truck is going to be full of large, irritated cops. I'm visiting the hospital tonight to tell him.'

'Wash your hands afterwards,' said Thane.

He said goodbye, hung up, and went back to prowling the police station again, digesting what he'd been told about the Glendirk set-up. From the tangle of loose ends that had gradually accumulated to the positive weave of what had to be the ultimate pattern had needed only a few final, anchoring strands.

It was a pattern which still had one or two small gaps. But its centre was complete – twenty-two kilos of amphetamine could leave Garrett rich and independent, able to throw aside his role as an all-round loser. The money would come soiled from gutter misery, but Thane doubted if that would have any place on the balance sheet.

The waiting dragged on, the radio stayed silent. Twice he was on the brink of calling up Francey Dunbar to find out what was going on, twice he stopped himself because he knew how he would have felt if their roles had been reversed. Sergeant Henderson brought in more coffee and, seeing the signs, wisely left him alone.

Then, at last, the radio did crackle to life.

'Wrapped up for now,' reported Dunbar laconically. 'I'm coming in.'

He arrived in the police station five minutes later, looking pleased with himself, accompanied by Sandra Craig. The red-haired girl was eating doughnuts from a paper bag, and kept on eating as she followed them through into Henderson's office.

'Well?' demanded Thane.

'This time, we were lucky,' said Dunbar, with a grin at the girl.

Thane listened while the story came straight, without embroidery.

When Benodet's small team had left the motel, using both cars, Dunbar had taken the gamble that they'd stay together. He'd sent Joe Felix and Sandra on their tail, using the Mini-Cooper, while he'd used the manager's pass-key for a quick check inside the vacant chalet.

It had been a waste of time. He'd found nothing. But thanks to the radio link between the two S.C.S. cars and some fast driving he'd managed to join Felix and the girl again at a parking area in the Aviemore Centre.

By then, they were watching just one car, the hired grey Fiat. Benodet had left his dark blue Jaguar in another of the Centre's parking areas, had joined Miriam Vassa and Coshy Jackton in the Fiat, and had made almost a complete circle before parking it.

When they left the car, Felix and Sandra Craig had followed, with Francey Dunbar keeping a low profile to the rear. Suddenly, after a short distance, Benodet and his bodyguard had halted and Miriam Vassa had continued on her own.

'Felix left her to Sandra and stayed clear,' said Dunbar. He rubbed his drooping moustache and chuckled. 'That's why I said we were lucky. There's no way Felix or any man could have managed to stick with the Vassa woman – you want to tell it, Sandra?'

She shook her head, licking sugar from her fingers and reaching into the bag for another doughnut.

'Fine.' Dunbar was enjoying himself. 'By then, they were near the fountain in the middle of the Centre, and that's a pretty busy spot. But straight off we spotted Joan Harton waiting beside the fountain –'

'What about Garrett?' demanded Thane. 'He went with her.'

Dunbar shook his head. 'If he was there, he stayed well back, and there were plenty of people around, sir. Anyway, the Vassa woman went up to Joan Harton, spoke to her and they walked from there into the nearest hotel and – well –' He glanced despairingly at the redhead.

'And they went into the ladies' powder room, so I went too,' said Sandra Craig with a touch of amusement. She shrugged. 'That's where they talked. I just locked myself in and caught a word here and there – tiled walls and plumbing don't make for good acoustics, sir.'

'I'll take your word for it,' said Thane. 'Well?'

She frowned. 'There's some sort of real meeting set for tonight. Benodet is to drive to a road junction, then they'll pick up a guide, and he'll take them on from there. The junction is at a place called Fiddlers something, a name like that anyway. I couldn't catch more.'

'We should be able to pin it down.' Thane pursed his lips, knowing they'd already got more than he'd hoped, but with another aspect nagging at his mind. 'Was Sean Russell mentioned?'

'If he was, I didn't hear it.' Sandra Craig shook her head. 'Most of the time I couldn't make out what was going on. I'm only sure about the meeting because they got into some kind of hassle about the details and Joan Harton said them again, like she was laying down the law.'

155

Thane nodded and lit a cigarette, hiding his disappointment. The bag of doughnuts finished, the girl squashed it into a tight ball and tossed it into a waste basket. As it landed, Francey Dunbar made a throat-clearing noise to get Thane's attention.

'Do we wait for tonight?' he asked.

'Yes, if it's going to lead us to that amphetamine,' said Thane grimly. 'What about Benodet now? Is he back at the motel?'

'With Joe Felix keeping an eye on him,' nodded Dunbar. 'And they're down to one car, the Jaguar, which makes life easier. When Joan Harton left, we stuck with the Vassa woman. She went back with Benodet and Jackton to the Fiat, but they simply drove it round to where the Jaguar was parked, then switched cars and abandoned the Fiat.'

'Shaking any tail,' mused Sandra Craig. 'They don't take chances.' She hesitated. 'Sir, Joe Felix reckons he could put a homer device on the Jaguar –'

Thane raised a surprised eyebrow. 'Did he bring one with him?'

She chuckled. 'He brought a suitcase full of electronic hardware. Joe feels naked without his bits and pieces.'

Twenty minutes later a stocky, balding man in gardening overalls began a lazy tidying of the ground around the motel chalets. He carried a black plastic sack and hummed a tune as he picked up scraps of litter and the occasional beer can. When he reached the place where Frank Benodet's Jaguar was parked he stopped and leaned against it for a moment, lighting a cigarette.

156

In the process, he dropped his matches. Stooping down, he picked them up again from the ground, and while doing so he placed a small, magnet grip homer device, not much bigger than the matchbox, under the metal of the Jaguar's rear bumper.

Then, unhurriedly, Joe Felix moved on and spent another few minutes picking up rubbish before he called it a day.

Watching from the strip of woodland which overlooked the line of chalets, Colin Thane flicked the switch of the receiver unit which Felix had given him. Two needle dials immediately quivered to life, one registering signal strength and the other direction.

The homer was operating. Felix had told him the unit had a battery life of twenty hours and a range of up to two miles. He turned the unit in his hands, saw the dials shift to new readings, and remembered the rest of what the S.C.S. surveillance man had said. For pinpoint accuracy two receiver units were needed, working sufficiently apart to give cross-bearings. But in mountain country the options were cut back and anyway they only had one unit available. It would give them a guide and it would have to do.

He switched off, handed the unit to Francey Dunbar, and walked back through the trees to where Sergeant Henderson was waiting in the Ford. Henderson had wanted to come along and had made a pallid excuse about 'needing a breath of air'.

'Does it work?' asked Henderson as Thane got in.

Thane nodded.

'I get nervous tension changing a fuse.' The grey-haired sergeant shook his head in an instinctive distrust of technology. 'Still, I've an idea now about the road junction where they're meeting. That policewoman of yours got it wrong, sir, the place is Fedlas, not Fiddlers. Fedlas crossroads is about four miles north-east of us, on the Nethy road.' He paused and frowned. 'Mind you, there's damn little there except trees and a tourist picnic area.'

'That's what they'd want.' Thane glanced at his watch. In another four hours it would be dusk. The action could start any time after that. 'What's the country like beyond there?'

'More trees, rock slopes, and a cottage or two.' Henderson shrugged. 'You're more likely to meet a deer than a human.' He rubbed his chin thoughtfully. 'Maybe I'd better come along with you, just in case your magic box goes wrong.'

'I was going to ask that,' said Thane. He chewed his lip for a moment, considering. They had a watch on Benodet at the chalet, another watch on Garrett's people at the distillery. They still had to guard against the unexpected, but otherwise all they had to do now was wait. 'Let's get back to your place, Sergeant. Then we can sort out some details.'

Four hours was a long time, much longer than a mere two hundred and forty minutes. Now and again a check call came into the little police station from the men on watch at either the motel or the distillery. Francey Dunbar made a trip out to the Ironbridge Hotel, collected their overnight bags, and paid the bill for the rooms – just in case anyone was inquisitive in that direction.

At 5 p.m. Robin Garrett drove from the distillery to his home, using his Volvo. Twenty minutes after that Margaret Garrett left the house at the wheel of a small

M.G. sports car on her journey to Edinburgh. Half an hour later a Northern Constabulary patrol car, deliberately idling well down the A9 trunk road, reported the M.G. heading south at speed.

Then, taking the watchers by surprise, Garrett returned to the distillery and left again almost immediately with Joan Harton in the passenger seat. Tailing them out came an old four-wheel-drive Land Rover with a canvas top. The Volvo turned west, towards Aviemore, the Land Rover headed in the opposite direction.

Listening in the police radio room, Thane accepted the situation unemotionally as both vehicles were lost from sight. He had half-expected it to happen. He was ready to wager that the Land Rover driver had been Shug MacLean, probably with Pete Stanson aboard. But he was taking a calculated risk in letting them go and keeping his real hopes pinned on Benodet.

Getting up from his seat, he walked over to the window where Francey Dunbar stood chewing gum and making a poor job of trying to look unconcerned. Outside, the light was beginning to grey with the first fine shading of approaching dusk. The sky was clear, which meant there should be reasonable moonlight. That would help.

'Anything special worrying you?' he asked Dunbar.

'No, sir.' Dunbar kept looking out of the window, but grimaced. 'The last cop who was teamed with you got a stomach ulcer, didn't he?'

'Correction, he had it from the start.' Thane grinned at the thought. 'All right, make sure the others are ready. We'll give it another ten minutes, then move out.'

Dunbar gave a relieved nod and headed for the

door. Then he stopped and glanced back, seemed ready to say something, but shook his head instead and went out.

It was 7 p.m. when Thane and Dunbar reached the Fedlas crossroads. They got out of their Ford, leaving Sergeant Henderson behind the wheel and Joe Felix grinning at them from the front passenger seat. Then, as the car drove off, Thane shrugged at Francey Dunbar, who was carrying a walkie-talkie radio and a pair of night glasses.

Henderson had said there wasn't much at Fedlas crossroads and Henderson had been right. A few wooden benches and a rubbish bin on a cleared patch of flattened earth constituted the picnic area. The rest was a plantation of young pine trees barely the height of a man, some scrub and gorse, and a patch of shallow bogland which they blundered into almost immediately.

Two hours later, cold and stiff, sheltering behind an outcrop of rock, Thane shivered in the cold north-east wind and drew only a slender consolation from the fact that Francey Dunbar, sheltering beside him, looked equally miserable in the pale moonlight.

Thane had the night glasses, Dunbar still nursed the radio. A half mile or so back down the road Joe Felix and Sergeant Henderson had the Ford hidden in an old quarry site. A Northern Constabulary patrol van was there too, with four constables aboard. Which left Sandra Craig with the Mini-Cooper, on her own apart from the radio link, to tail Benodet's Jaguar when it left the motel.

The Jaguar had left there five minutes earlier and was coming their way. Frank Benodet was in the rear seat with Miriam Vassa and his bodyguard Jackton

160

was driving. The message had come crackling in over the walkie-talkie and was the first real news they'd had. In the two hours of waiting the total traffic through the crossroads had amounted to a handful of cars, a solitary truck, and the local mail van.

'Can't be long now,' murmured Dunbar, easing back on his heels in a crunch of gravelly soil.

Thane nodded, then gave a warning grunt and brought the night glasses up to his eyes. A glow of light was coming towards them on the road to their right. A moment later it became a motor cycle, the headlamp a single glaring eye, engine throttled down to a purr.

The machine slowed to a crawl, then stopped in the middle of the crossroads, engine ticking over. The rider, in dark leather and a crash helmet, looked around. Then the machine's engine revved and it circled, going back the way it had come.

'So Stanson's the guide,' said Dunbar as the motor cycle's tail light vanished round a bend.

'It looks that way.' Thane lowered the glasses. It had certainly been Stanson's trail bike and he guessed it had come out of the distillery in the back of the Land Rover. 'Tell Henderson.'

Dunbar spoke into the radio, received a brief acknowledgement, and they settled down to their shivering vigil again. Somewhere out among the trees a small animal screamed as it fell prey to something larger. Then car headlights showed, coming along the road from Aviemore.

The Jaguar reached the crossroads a minute later, coasted to a halt at the verge about fifty yards short of the junction, and waited with sidelights on and a soft throb coming from its exhaust. The driver lit a

161

cigarette, a red pinpoint glow in the darkened interior where the three occupants were just vague shapes in the night.

Dunbar was muttering into the radio again when the motor cycle returned. This time it made a wide sweep through the crossroads and swung round to halt beside the Jaguar. Then after a moment's conversation between rider and driver the motor cycle snarled off, once again taking the road to the right with the Jaguar following, headlights blazing.

'Sergeant Henderson's on his way,' said Dunbar, lowering the radio. He gave a mirthless grin. 'So far, it's working out.'

Thane nodded, and they moved out towards the road.

Headlights came towards them. Henderson and Joe Felix arrived first, with the Ford, then Sandra Craig just beat the following patrol van into second place, bringing the S.C.S. Mini-Cooper to a skidding halt. Thane got into the back seat of the Ford, saw Francey Dunbar getting aboard the Mini-Cooper as they'd arranged, then the little convoy started off again and turned right at the crossroads, beginning their shadowing.

'Got them?' he asked Felix, who had the homer receiver unit on his lap.

'About two thirds of a mile ahead,' answered Felix absently, his attention fixed on the twin dials. 'There's some signal fluctuation, but that's normal.'

'Good.' Thane switched his attention to Henderson. 'We want to keep the gap. But what about this road?'

'I know it.' Henderson spared a moment to check his rear view mirror for the other two vehicles, which were driving on sidelights only. 'Runs fairly straight through the hills between here and joins the Cairngorm road, sir. About the only tracks running off it are forestry service roads.'

They drove on at the same steady pace along the otherwise empty ribbon of moonlit tarmac with the trees and rocks on either side mere gaunt, black silhouettes against the night. Then, after a couple of miles, Felix gave a sudden grunt and peered intently at his receiver unit.

'They've turned right,' he declared. 'About half a mile ahead, no more. May be slowing down a bit too, sir. I can't be sure.'

'One of the forestry roads,' said Henderson, then gave a chuckle. 'Yes, I remember it – and it makes sense. There's an abandoned sawmill up there. Maybe that's the place they've been using, Superintendent.'

They reached the start of the forestry road, swung off the tarmac route, and began lurching along a dirt and gravel surface. Grimacing, Henderson switched off the Ford's headlights, slowed the car to not much more than a crawl, and hunched forward over the steering wheel. Peering ahead, relying on the moonlight and memory, he began muttering under his breath, talking to the car, nursing it on while the forestry road began to climb.

Thane stayed silent, knowing that was the best way to help. Now and again the whole car shuddered as they clipped a rock or bucked through an unseen pothole. Behind them, the Mini-Cooper and the patrol van had begun to fall behind.

Then, unexpectedly, Joe Felix said, 'Something's wrong. I've a signal bearing left, increasing that way.'

'Then your damned contraption is wrong,' snapped Henderson, concentrating ahead. 'This is the sawmill road.'

'Can't help that,' said Felix. 'Still bearing left, angle and distance increasing.'

Suddenly Henderson swore and brought the Ford to a juddering halt. His face bitter in the moonlight, he swung round to face Thane.

'There's a left fork not far back,' he said wearily. 'Don't ask me why the hell they've gone that way. It's a service route, pure and simple – nothing up there but trees and more damned trees. But if that's the way they've gone –'

'Still reading left,' said Felix impassively.

They reversed. Which meant the Mini-Cooper and the patrol van had to do the same, inching back down the track with painstaking care. The fork came up, almost hidden in the trees.

'What range?' demanded Thane.

'About a mile, direct bearing,' said Felix. He shrugged. 'It must be a pretty winding stretch of road.'

'It is,' said Henderson bleakly.

They started crawling forward again, on the new road. It climbed even more steeply than the previous route and Henderson occasionally had to resort to the headlamps when a rising bluff of rock or a steep hillside meant they plunged into dark shadow. Diplomatically Felix said nothing more for several minutes. Then he turned in his seat and frowned unhappily at Thane.

'What's wrong?' asked Thane.

'No signal. Hell, I don't understand it, sir. The receiver unit's functioning. Either the homer's failed or –' He stopped there and let his voice trail away, shaking his head again.

'All right.' Thane clenched his fists for a moment,

then took the only decision he could. 'Let's find out, Sergeant.'

Henderson nodded. The Ford's headlights blazed to life, the car accelerated sharply, and gravel and small stones spat out from beneath their tyres as they began speeding along the dirt road. A bend came up, and the elderly sergeant dropped down a gear, and took it in skidding, almost rally style.

There was another bend just ahead and Henderson tackled it in the same way. Clutching for support in the rear, Thane saw the Mini-Cooper and the patrol van left far behind. They bounced on, Felix still reporting no signal, one tree-lined bend succeeding another, the road always climbing, then suddenly their headlights showed a timber bridge ahead, and at the same instant Henderson cried a startled warning and jammed on the brakes as hard as he could.

Brakes screaming, the Ford went into a skidding uncontrollable sideways slide, and at the same instant Thane felt a moment of raw, naked fear.

The bridge was down. The centre section was just a black gap framed by broken timbers, one side-rail gone.

They slid on, swinging violently as the car's tail slammed a rock, shuddering on its springs. Then somehow they had stopped, almost broadside to the bridge and only a few feet away from the start of its planking.

'God Almighty,' said Joe Felix shakily. He licked his lips, staring in horror, unable to find anything else to say.

Henderson had slumped back into his seat. But he came to life again and followed as Thane stumbled out of the car. Going forward together, they reached

165

the edge of the gap and stared down into the deep rock gorge spanned by the broken bridge with the sound of rushing water loud in their ears.

Down there, the night was black – except for one faint patch of diffused, oddly quivering light far below.

Staring down, Thane fought down a wave of nausea as he realized what it was. The Jaguar was down there, under water, and the glow was one of its headlamps still shining beneath the surface. That was why they had lost the homer signal, that was why the bridge was wrecked – but how had it happened? He shoved that out of his mind and faced Henderson, whose elderly face was a stony, waiting mask.

'We've got to get down to them,' said Thane.

'Aye.' Henderson nodded slowly. His eyes strayed past Thane to the road. The Mini-Cooper and the patrol van were halting behind the Ford, lights blazing, their occupants spilling out. 'But I'm not letting anyone go rushing, not you or anyone else, Superintendent. That's a long way down and we'll do it right – the way my lads are trained.' He shrugged. 'Put one foot wrong on the way and you could break your neck – and anyone in that car is dead by now.'

Thane surrendered to the cold logic in the man's words. Then, as Henderson began giving orders and his men produced ropes and hand-torches from the patrol van, he turned back alone to the bridge.

In his mind he was picturing the motor cycle and the following car coming through the night towards the bridge, reaching it with headlights blazing. And then – he frowned at the bridge, considering it carefully, shutting his mind to the noisy activity behind him.

The bridge had been built in a simple, sturdy style.

Thick planks of wood like railway sleepers, laid side by side, had been spiked down on to the basic frame-work of the structure. On the far side of the gap, a broken sleeper hung drunkenly from the last twisted spike which held it.

But on his side there was a clean ending. Nothing remained, not even a broken remnant of spike –

'Sir?' Sandra Craig's voice, quiet but concerned, made him turn. She moistened her lips. 'I – can I help?'

She had a torch. He nodded, took the torch from her, and knelt down to examine the last sleeper before the gap. There were distinct marks on the wood which told their own story of how a lever had been at work, how the gap had been made.

Benodet had been cold-bloodedly led into a trap, blindly following his motor cycle guide. Except how had the guide escaped?

Ignoring the girl's puzzled frown, he moved delib-erately to the centre of the timber decking, then worked his way back slowly from the edge. He found what he'd half-expected three feet back from the gap – a cluster of small, fresh nail-holes on the rough surface. One nail still remained, with a fragment of ordinary white wood planking around the head.

'That's how they did it,' he said, turning back to Sandra Craig again. 'First they make a gap, then they bridge it again, but just enough for a rider who knows it's there to get his machine across. Then the car comes –' he slapped a fist viciously into his opened hand – 'straight through, takes the thing away with it.' He drew a deep breath. 'Where's Francey?'

'Over there.' She gestured to their side of the gorge, where Henderson's men now had ropes snaking down under the glare of a powerful emergency spot-light. 'He's going down.'

'No, he's not. Get him here – and Sergeant Hender-son.' Hands in his pockets, Thane waited till Dunbar and Henderson hurried over. From their expressions, Sandra Craig had told them enough to stop them ask-ing questions. For the moment, that was how Thane wanted it. He asked Henderson, 'What happens to this road, on the other side?'

'It's like I said, just a service road.' Henderson scraped a hand along his chin. 'As I remember, it takes a wide loop and comes back out on the Nethy road. But –'

'Right.' Thane cut him short and swung towards Dunbar. 'Francey, take Felix and Sandra and one of the cars. Get back to Aviemore, collect any uniformed help you can get, then pull in Garrett's bunch, any you can find. No arguments, no discussion – just haul them in, and I don't care how. Understand?'

'Yes.' Francey Dunbar looked past him at the black gap in the bridge and his mouth tightened for an instant. 'Suppose they've skipped?'

'Then go looking for them,' Thane said. He turned back to Henderson again. 'You're going down?'

Henderson nodded.

'I'm coming with you,' said Thane.

Henderson didn't argue. They walked together towards the dangling ropes while Francey Dunbar collected Joe Felix and hurried him to where Sandra Craig was starting up the Mini-Cooper.

Chapter Seven

Even with the ropes, it was a long, harsh scramble down the face of the gorge under the glare of the spotlight. Clawing scrub and sharp edges of rock added discomfort to danger and Colin Thane was glad when he got to the bottom. He joined Henderson and two of the uniformed constables on a narrow ledge with a foaming river a noisy torrent just below their feet.

'Careful,' warned Henderson. 'That water's damned deep, ice-cold off the mountains, and you'd have to run to keep up with the current.'

Thane nodded. They were on the up-stream side of the wooden bridge, a thin silhouette high above them in the night sky. But down at their level the eerie gleam from the submerged car's solitary headlamp, a gleam that was already starting to weaken, remained all that really mattered.

'Suppose someone got out?' he asked.

'Then dead or alive they'll be a long way downstream,' said Henderson, then sighed. 'I've radioed for help and we'll need it. But maybe we can make a start.'

He left Thane and talked quietly to one of the constables for a moment. Then while the other constable climbed back up the gorge and returned with a coil of thin rope and a waterproof torch, the first man stripped off his clothes.

They knotted one end of the rope around his waist and secured the other end to a projection of rock. Grimacing, the torch held tightly in one hand, the constable plunged into the torrent and struck out strongly, fighting out towards midstream as the current swept him along. Then, as he neared the glow in the water, he dived down.

An age seemed to pass before the man surfaced again and shouted. Hastily Thane pulled on the rope to help him fight against the current, back to the ledge, where the constable clambered out, quivering with cold and exhaustion.

'Here, lad.' Quickly, Henderson wrapped his own heavy coat round the swimmer, ignoring the water dripping from the man's body. 'Well?'

'They're inside, all three of them,' said the constable through chattering teeth. He looked at Thane. 'The car's lying on its side, sir, in about fifteen feet o' water, and it's pretty badly smashed up.' He paused and drew gratefully on the lighted cigarette Thane put between his lips.

'There's a window half-opened at the rear, as if someone made a try at getting out, but –' He left it at that, and shook his head.

'Right. Get dressed and out of this.' Thane turned to Henderson. 'There's a bottle of whisky in the Ford. He's earned a stiff treble.'

Henderson nodded.

'Wait, sir,' said the man awkwardly. 'There's – well, there's another body down there.'

'What the hell do you mean?' demanded Henderson, startled. 'You said there were three in the car, so –'

'In it, yes.' The constable pulled the coat tighter round his shoulders, shivering violently, then turned appealingly to Thane. 'There's another body, caught up in the bodywork on the outside, sir. A man – I just caught a glimpse of him, then I had to surface.'

'You're sure?' asked Thane curtly.

'I saw him,' persisted the constable.

Henderson sent the constable towards his clothing, then faced Thane, frowning. 'It must be Stanson. His riding the plank stunt must have come unstuck.'

'Yes.' Thane looked at the turbulent river water for a moment. The glow from the headlamp was fading fast, the practical thing was to wait till proper recovery gear arrived. But a terrible doubt was creeping into his mind. He drew a deep breath. 'I want that rope, Sergeant, and the torch.'

Ignoring Henderson's protests, he stripped quickly, fastened the rope round his waist as the constable had done, and took the torch. It had a short lanyard which he slipped round his wrist. Then he went into the river.

The cold hit him like a solid wall, several times worse than he'd expected. Gasping, Thane struck out against the current, battled towards midstream as he was swept down towards the bridge, saw the glow ahead, and dived down.

His torch and the glow from the headlamp guided him in. A moment later he grabbed the side of the Jaguar, then found himself looking in through the driver's window. Jackton lay pinned behind the steering wheel. Behind him, Benodet and the woman were an obscene, limp tangle, the woman's dark hair moving as if alive in the current snatching in through the half-opened window.

171

But that wasn't what he'd come for. Hand-holding his way along, Thane reached the rear of the car. The luggage boot lid had burst open, one edge jammed against the river bed, a dark shape lying half in and half out of it. He clawed nearer, brought the torch-beam close, and it shone on a man's lifeless, staring eyes and slack, opened mouth.

It wasn't Stanson. The man had fair hair, a young face, a leather jacket, and his wrists were tied together. He'd found Sean Russell.

Sickened, his lungs close to bursting, Thane let go of the car, and kicked upwards. He broke surface, the rope tightening round his waist as the current grabbed and tried to drag him along. He shouted, and the men on the ledge began to pull him in.

Afterwards, Colin Thane had only a hazy recollection of how he was dried down with an old rag of a towel produced from somewhere, of fumbling back into his clothes then, every limb feeling frozen to the bone, of clawing his way back up to the top of the gorge.

The constable who'd plunged into the river before him was still inside the Ford. He passed Thane the opened whisky bottle without a word and the fiery, overproof spirit blazed a path down his throat, then seemed to explode in his stomach.

In a little while he had recovered physically though what he'd seen under the river was imprinted in his mind like a series of photographs from a portfolio of horror. Henderson came back up and talked to him. Soon after that another police patrol van arrived with more men and more equipment. Two of the men were from a police rescue team and had black rubber skin-diving suits and scuba gear.

Most of the time Thane stayed by his car, his face an iron-hard mask that discouraged company and hid a sick revulsion at what he'd seen.

Four more deaths. He tortured himself with the thought that it might not have happened if he'd acted differently, if he hadn't planned his whole strategy around using Benodet to lead him to the narcotics. Yet had there been another way, one with any chance of success?

All that came to him by way of an answer was the picture of Sean Russell's vacant, staring eyes in that underwater horror and the way the young skiing instructor's wrists had been tied together. To be in that luggage boot, helpless, trapped, as the Jaguar took her plunge into the river – Thane's stomach tightened at the thought.

Benodet had held Russell as a prisoner for at least twenty-four hours. Most, if not all, of that time he must have been in the luggage boot, cramped and probably terrified. Then, at the end, whether they'd known or cared, it had been his own friends who had cold-bloodedly sacrificed him.

But it could have been different – again and again the thought forced its way into Thane's mind. He wasn't sure how much time had passed when Sergeant Henderson appeared again.

'We're getting the first of the bodies out now,' reported Henderson. He eyed Thane warily. 'Uh – are you feeling all right, sir?'

Thane nodded absently. As Henderson turned away, a car growled up the track and stopped. It was the S.C.S. Mini-Cooper and Francey Dunbar was aboard, alone. Getting out, Dunbar spoke to Henderson first, then came over.

'Sorry, sir.' The young sergeant shook his head sadly as he reached Thane. 'No go. Garrett, the Harton woman, MacLean, Stanson – not a trace of them.' He paused and grimaced hopefully. 'But I don't think they've totally skipped, not yet, anyway.' He stopped again, considered Thane closely, and gave a concerned grunt. 'You look rough. Henderson told me –'

'Damn Henderson,' said Thane curtly. 'You think they haven't totally skipped. Why?'

Dunbar shrugged. 'It adds up that way. There's a suitcase lying packed in Joan Harton's house. We dragged MacLean's wife out of bed, and as far as she's concerned he's working night-shift, but he told her he'd have to go away in the morning, checking some plant down south that Garrett wants to buy – and Garrett's Volvo is lying in one of the Aviemore car parks.'

'All right. Tell it straight next time.' Thane stared past Dunbar into the night. 'Are we ready for them if they show?'

'All round,' nodded Dunbar. 'A Northern Constabulary detective inspector and a C.I.D. squad came rolling in – Henderson's boss was getting worried. I left them to it and – well, came back.'

But Garrett had to be getting ready to pull out. Thane stayed staring into the night. Garrett and his companions were out there somewhere, with only one possible reason now. Before they vanished from Speyside they had to collect the amphetamine, perhaps take time to destroy the last traces of its manufacture.

They were out there. But where, in that vast sprawling wilderness of hills?

'They'll show,' said Dunbar confidently, as if reading his mind.

'Maybe.' Thane drew a deep breath, knowing there was one thing he could do, had to do. 'Keep checking. I'm going to see Angus Russell. Someone has to tell him.'

'I could come along,' said Dunbar, frowning. 'I mean –'

'When I need help, I'll ask for it,' snapped Thane. 'I told you to keep checking. Do that.'

He got into the Ford, started it up, and turned it viciously on the narrow track. Standing watching, Dunbar shook his head as the car drove off. Then he went over to talk to Henderson again.

It was almost 3 a.m. when Angus Russell answered Thane's knocking on the door of his cottage. The small, leathery-skinned photographer's eyes were bleary with sleep, he wore a tattered old dressing gown over pyjamas, but from the moment he fumbled the door open and saw Thane it was as if he knew.

They went in together into the same untidy room. Then, without a word, Russell went straight to where he kept his whisky bottle and glasses, poured two stiff drinks with trembling hands, and brought them back.

'Here.' He handed Thane one of the glasses and took a gulp at his own. When he spoke again, there was a total sad resignation in his voice. 'It's about Sean, isn't it?'

'Yes,' said Thane simply.

'Aye.' Russell moistened his lips. 'And you wouldn't come to my door at this hour unless –'

'He's dead,' agreed Thane softly. 'I'm sorry.'

175

Blindly Russell set down his half-empty glass and turned away. For a long moment he stood with his head bowed, his hands resting on the top of his cluttered desk. When he turned again, he brushed a bundle of photographs on to the floor but ignored them. Suddenly his face was that of an old, tired man.

'How did it happen?' he asked.

'He was in a car. It – well it went through a bridge up in the hills, into a river,' said Thane gravely. 'We were following, though they didn't know that. By the time we got there, there was nothing anyone could have done.'

Russell nodded wearily. Crossing over, he slumped down into one of the battered chairs.

'Who else was with him?' he asked.

'People from London.' Thane hesitated, but knew he had to go on. 'None of his friends, and it wasn't an accident.'

Russell stared up at him. 'You mean –'

'His friends wrote him off,' said Thane deliberately. 'You knew he was up to his neck in trouble, didn't you?'

Russell nodded, closed his eyes, and sat with his bald head bowed against his chest. A single trickle of a tear ran down one cheek. Thane waited, the untouched drink still in his hand, hating what he was having to do but knowing there was no alternative.

'He was a damn fool,' said Russell in a low voice at last, looking up again. 'He had his chances, you know. He really did and he could have made it –' He shook his head bitterly. 'A man's son stays his son, Superintendent. I thought – hell, it doesn't matter what I thought, not now. But I knew he was mixed up in something, even before you arrived.'

176

'Asking some of the right questions but mostly getting the wrong answers,' agreed Thane.

Russell nodded. 'Yes, I tried to steer you off. Then I – well, I tried to find Sean, last night and most of today. But –' He shrugged resignedly and sucked his lips. 'Him and his pal Stanson – and what's the rest of it? Garrett and the distillery? You wouldn't tell me before, but now – man, I'd say I've a right to know.'

'You have,' answered Thane. He took a sip from his drink, forming what he wanted to say. 'But there's also a reason. The same people killed your son. Maybe they didn't know it, maybe they did, but they killed him.'

'And I want to know why,' said Russell unsteadily.

'A string of armed hold-ups and a million pounds' worth of drugs,' said Thane. He saw Russell's mouth fall open in bewildered disbelief and nodded grimly. 'I'll tell you some of it – enough so you'll understand.'

He did. Listening, Russell seemed to gradually sag lower and lower in the old armchair and Thane pitied him, yet daren't relent. But at last he finished. He had skirted briefly round the way he'd been using Benodet and had missed out altogether any knowledge of Sean Russell being held as a hostage. It left that part of the story weak, but Angus Russell didn't seem to notice.

'I'm grateful to you.' Russell spoke in not much above a whisper. 'If I'd known, even guessed it was that bad –' He stopped, shook his head, then for the first time an angry glint showed in his eyes. 'So where are they now, Garrett and the others?'

'You might know.' Quickly Thane raised a hand to stop the older man's protest. 'Think about it. There has to be a place somewhere out there in the hills,

177

a place your son knew about – somewhere safe enough to set up a laboratory and secure enough to leave unguarded.'

'You're talking about more than a hundred square miles of near emptiness,' said Russell wearily. 'Man, I've tramped around for days out there and not seen another living soul.'

'Then let's try and make it easier,' urged Thane. He filled Russell's glass from the whisky bottle and took the drink over to him. 'I reckon it has to be a hut or a cottage of some kind and that it has to be reasonably close to – well, at least a track that a vehicle could use. Try and remember anything that Sean might have said to you, anything that might have given you some kind of a hint.'

Pensively scowling, Russell sipped at the whisky, then shook his head.

'None I can remember. He came to see me now and again, but there was never much talk between us.'

'What about places he'd been, even things he'd seen,' persisted Thane. 'Think hard.'

'I'm trying.' The leathery face twisted in concentration. Then, suddenly, Russell swore under his breath, set down his glass so hastily some of the liquor slopped over the rim, and got up. Crossing to the desk, he pawed urgently through the stacks of photographs, ignoring the prints on the floor. At last he found what he wanted, stared at it hard for a moment, then said quietly, 'There's always this.'

Thane came over. The man was holding a colour photograph of a line of deer crossing a hill, the lead stag silhouetted against the sky. It was good without being spectacular.

'Picture postcard stuff,' admitted Russell. 'It's from

178

a batch I took about a month ago.' He sucked his lips. 'When I showed this one to Sean, he made a fuss about wanting to know where I'd been. But – well, the moment I told him I'd been west of here, over towards Cain Dulnan, he wasn't interested any more.'

'Suppose he was worried because it might have been somewhere else,' suggested Thane hopefully. 'Give that a try.'

'That's the notion I've been thinking about,' said Russell slowly, frowning at the print. 'The shape of the hill could have thrown him. There's one like it to the east of here, in the high country towards Glen Avon. It's a damned lonely part of the world, except –'

'Well?' Thane couldn't curb his impatience.

'There's an old shooting lodge close by, not much more than a cottage.' Russell drew a deep breath and glanced at Thane. 'An English family had it as a holiday home, but there was a story they'd sold it a few months ago. There's a track of sorts that would let a man drive almost to the door, if he knew how to get there and had something like my Land Rover.'

'It's a possibility,' said Thane softly. 'We haven't got a better one.'

'You'll need a guide,' said Russell, his voice hoarse. Thane nodded.

'Thank you.' Putting down the photograph, Russell straightened and gave a bitter smile. 'Give me ten minutes to get some clothes on.'

He reappeared in less than that time, dressed in his heavy breeches and climbing boots, the sheepskin waistcoat flapping loose over his thick wool shirt. As if from habit, the small, stocky figure started towards the camera lying on top of the desk. Then he stopped, shrugged, picked up his blue beret instead, and led the way towards the door.

The night seemed pitch-black when they went outside. Then, as Russell closed the cottage door, Thane saw a figure leaning against the side of his Ford. It was Francey Dunbar, who stayed exactly as he was, hands in his pockets, as Thane strode over.

'What the hell are you doing here?' demanded Thane.

'Waiting for you.' Dunbar said it casually and gestured beyond the car. 'We – uh – felt it might be a good idea.'

The Mini-Cooper was parked a short stone's throw away, the shadowy figures of Sandra Craig and Joe Felix standing beside it.

'The local cops are taking care of things,' added Dunbar conversationally, and gave an almost embarrassed shrug. 'Anyway –'

'All right.' Thane swallowed, then cleared his throat heavily, understanding what Dunbar really meant and touched by the way all three were there. He covered up his feelings curtly. 'I can use you. We may have a lead to where Garrett is.'

Dunbar gave a surprised whistle, then looked in Angus Russell's direction.

'He's our guide,' agreed Thane. He saw the other question coming and nodded. 'I told him about his son. This is his idea, and we're using his Land Rover.'

'There's a happy thought,' muttered Dunbar. 'Do we tell the local troops?'

'Just that we're going – Russell will tell you where,' said Thane. 'Radio in, and say we'll let them know if we need any back-up later.'

'Amen,' agreed Dunbar and headed towards where Russell was standing impatiently.

They left a few minutes later, Angus Russell driving his old Land Rover, Thane up beside him, and the other three crammed into the rear. At that hour, the Aviemore Centre was deserted, a dark, sleeping silhouette in the night. Once past it, they stayed on the main road for about a mile without seeing another vehicle, then, with a warning grunt, Russell swung the wheel.

A moment later they were bumping and jarring over a narrow track that wound like a weed-encrusted snake in the headlamps' glare. Rattling over a cattle grid, engine grinding as Russell changed gear, the vehicle vibrated like the inside of a drum. Glancing round, Thane saw Felix hunched miserably, protecting the walkie-talkie set on his lap. Sandra Craig had jammed herself in a corner and Francey Dunbar had anchored himself to a metal stanchion.

'How long will it take us?' he asked Russell.

'An hour or so.' The photographer answered vaguely, his voice flat and his attention totally on his task behind the wheel. 'That's in daylight – I've never done it by night before.'

They bounced on a protruding boulder, Dunbar cursed in the back, and Thane tried again.

'Is it all like this?'

'This?' Russell glanced at him briefly with empty eyes. 'This is the easy bit.'

It was. The rough bottom land gave way to a strip of forest, then that in turn faded while the track began a gradual climb. The moon came out from behind a bank of clouds in time to show a silver glint of water below, on their right, and ahead nothing but a desolation of hills and rock, their route a barely discernible scratch across the surface. The Land Rover's progress dropped to not much more than walking pace, a four-wheel drive whine and snarl as Russell kept her shuddering on.

Senses dulled, Thane lost count of time. The occasional curse and muffled complaint from the back died away as despairing resignation took over. Only Russell seemed untouched, driving with a cold dedication and a face that was a grey mask in the pale moonlight.

And they kept climbing. Sounds faded, then returned in a roar as they cleared their ears air-travel style. The headlamp beams scattered a small herd of deer which had strayed across the track. Other, smaller wildlife occasionally scurried to safety and Russell broke his silence once, to grunt and nod as a strange mottled white bird rose almost vertically to escape their wheels.

It was a ptarmigan, Scotland's bird of the high places. To see one at all underlined their progress.

A minute later, the Land Rover bucked and slammed over still another rock, and a tyre blew. Swearing, Angus Russell clambered out as soon as they'd come to a halt. As the others followed him out, shivering in the frosty air, he scowled at the damage, then busied himself getting out the jack and spare.

'How far now?' asked Thane, helping him.

'From here?' Russell nodded at the black outline of a hogback hill ahead. 'That's the Cailleach – the Old Woman – and the shooting lodge is just the other side of it. A mile and a bit, no more.' He kicked the wrecked tyre viciously. 'So let's get this shifted.'

It was a fumbling, difficult job done by torchlight, the wheel nuts rusted and stubborn. Then, as they finished and Russell tossed the damaged wheel into the back of the Land Rover, Francey Dunbar grabbed Thane's arm.

'Over there,' he said softly, nodding ahead.

A pale glow of slowly moving light was coming towards them from the Cailleach hill, still far off but strengthening as they watched. While the others stared, Thane called Russell over.

'Could anyone else be on this track?' he demanded.

Russell shook his head, his mouth a tight, expectant line.

'They'll land right in our laps,' Francey Dunbar murmured happily. He turned to Thane. 'How will we play it?'

'Cool.' Thane looked around the raw, barren landscape, then stopped as he eyed a massive outcrop of rock which they'd barely passed before the tyre had blown. It gave him his answer. 'Cool, and a way they won't expect.' He turned to Russell. 'But it will need your Land Rover – and there's a risk in it for you.'

'If you're thinking of a wee ramming job, I'm ahead of you,' said Russell grimly. 'Let's stop wasting time and get ready.'

They had only minutes. The Land Rover's lights extinguished, the glow of the approaching headlights growing steadily nearer, they set to work. Guided by Thane, Angus Russell reversed his vehicle back beyond the outcrop and into its shelter and kept it there, the engine ticking over. Thane positioned Dunbar and Felix on the far side of the track, crouched

183

down in a patch of tangled heather, and Sandra Craig was several feet above his head, perched in hiding on the outcrop. She had a torch and a clear view along the track.

Standing beside the rock, Thane glanced again at Russell hunched behind the Land Rover's wheel. Then he took the Webley automatic from his pocket, checked the safety catch, and laid the gun on the cold rock beside him.

The glow of headlamps came nearer, then he could hear the labouring four-wheel-drive sound of another Land Rover and a rasp as the driver changed gear. The glow became a stab of light along the track and seconds later the shaded torch in Sandra Craig's hand blinked once from the outcrop, down towards Russell.

The murmur from Russell's vehicle became a growl. The torch blinked again and Thane tensed. Suddenly, the approaching vehicle was there, almost beside him, he saw the canvas top – and at the same instant Russell's Land Rover catapulted forward, headlamps glaring to life.

Metal crunched metal. Both Land Rovers stalled, locked together almost head-on, a smashed headlamp glass tinkling as it fell.

Gun in hand, Thane sprang towards the passenger door, conscious of Dunbar and Felix charging in from the driver's side. He wrenched the door open with his free hand, met Joan Harton's terrified eyes, and unceremoniously hauled her out.

Shouts, a crash as someone fell, then a warning yell came from the other side. Shoving Joan Harton against the vehicle's side, Thane swung round in time to see a figure sprinting round past the tailgate.

It was Shug MacLean, with Francey Dunbar in hot pursuit. Then another, slimmer figure intervened, coming down from the outcrop in a twisting, feet-first dive that took the burly distillery foreman square between the shoulders. MacLean dropped as if pole-axed and lay still while Sandra Craig rolled clear and sat up grinning as Dunbar reached her.

Angus Russell had tumbled out of his Land Rover. He shouldered Thane aside, glared at Joan Harton, and his hand came up to hit the trembling woman. Thane shoved between them again, blocking the blow, and Russell subsided, stepping back.

'I'll take her,' murmured Sandra Craig, appearing at Thane's elbow.

He let go and she spun Joan Harton round in expert style, pushing her bodily against the metal again. Thane checked the rear of the vehicle, found it was empty, and turned in time to hear the click as the woman's wrists were handcuffed behind her back. Dunbar had done the same to Shug MacLean and the distillery foreman had begun groaning as he was hauled into a sitting position.

'Where's Felix?' demanded Thane anxiously, looking around.

'Here,' said an unhappy voice. Holding his left shoulder tightly, wincing as he moved, Felix came round from the far side of the vehicles and scowled in MacLean's direction. 'This one hit me with the door – or it felt like it. And he made a try to get at a shotgun behind his seat.'

'Stand still,' said Angus Russell. He felt Felix's shoulder, who produced a yelp of pain, and grunted unsympathetically. 'Collarbone's broken – you could do worse playing football.'

185

'Who the hell wants to play football?' asked Felix despairingly.

'I can strap it up.' Ignoring him, Russell looked grimly at Thane. 'Well, you've got these two. But –'

'I know,' nodded Thane. 'Fix him up. I'll talk with what we've got.'

As Russell turned to tend to the injured detective, Thane beckoned Sandra Craig towards him. She came, shoving Joan Harton along with her.

'As for you,' he said dryly, 'you could have broken your neck. Nicely done, but don't try it again.'

'I'll ask first, sir,' she said, then pointed at Joan Harton. 'I think this one is coming out of shock.'

Thane faced the woman coldly. She had stopped trembling but there was enough light coming from the surviving headlamps to see the raw fear in her eyes.

'So which name do you prefer?' he asked caustically. 'The one you use here, or Marion Cooper, the one you used in Glasgow?' He saw her flinch but ignored her for a moment, signalling to Dunbar. 'Francey, check through their Land Rover. You know what we're looking for.'

Dunbar nodded and went off.

'Right.' Thane turned to the woman again. 'I haven't time to waste. I want Garrett and Stanson. Where are they?'

She moistened her lips. In the background, Shug MacLean snarled a warning.

'Keep your mouth shut,' he told her hoarsely. 'These bastards can't touch you.' Struggling to his feet, the handcuffs clinking behind his back, he glared defiantly at Thane. 'And I know a damned good lawyer.'

186

'You'll need him,' said Thane. Two steps took him across to the distillery foreman. Grabbing MacLean by the shirt-front, he pulled him closer. 'On the other hand, I've got Angus Russell with me. He knows his son is dead.' He saw MacLean's eyes widen and nodded. 'Benodet had him aboard the car – in the luggage boot. Didn't you know?'

'No, we –' MacLean stopped there, swallowing hard.

'Didn't you know or didn't you care?' Thane released his grip in disgust and pushed MacLean away. 'What did you do afterwards – pat each other on the back? Maybe I should tell that to Angus Russell, then leave you with him.'

'No.' MacLean's toughness evaporated at the thought. 'You're bluffin', you couldn't –'

'Don't tempt me,' warned Thane. 'We saw Stanson meet Benodet, we were following them.' He swung to Joan Harton again. 'The same way we were around when you went to Aviemore earlier and set it up.'

A muffled shout came from the Land Rover and he stopped as Francey Dunbar hurried over carrying a grubby airline flight bag.

'Jackpot,' he said happily. 'Take a look – this was under the front seats.'

Thane took the bag. Inside were four small, bulging plastic sacks. He opened one, felt the powdery contents, sniffed at a pinch, then carefully sealed the sack again. At a guess, the sacks held close on two kilos of amphetamine.

'Well?' he asked softly. 'What was this lot for – bus fares?'

'So we were gettin' out,' said MacLean bitterly, staring at the bag.

'You – with him?' Thane asked Joan Harton, glancing from her to the stocky distillery foreman.

'Just to the nearest airport,' she said in a low, weary voice.

'Where you'd split this?' Thane hefted the flight bag. 'What happened to the rest of it?'

She shrugged. 'We divided the last production run tonight, after –'

'After Benodet?'

MacLean swore to himself, then shoved forwards. 'Look, that was Pete Stanson's idea. Get that part straight, mister. Stanson suggested the bridge bit, Garrett liked it. We knew Sean might be with them, but that was his hard luck – that's what Garrett said.'

'We had to get rid of Benodet,' said Joan Harton. 'He wanted to take over, make us keep producing and buy the stuff cut-price.' She turned from Thane to Dunbar and Sandra Craig, who were standing silently, just listening. 'All we'd planned was a single operation – make our money, close down, get out. You can understand that, can't you?'

'I'm just a cop,' said Dunbar woodenly. 'I'm not supposed to understand things. But try it on a jury.'

Sandra Craig nudged him and grimaced. Joe Felix and Angus Russell were back, watching and listening. Felix's shoulder was tightly strapped with a bandage but Russell mattered more – in the glow of light his lined, leathery face was set like iron, a powder-keg of suppressed fury waiting to explode.

MacLean saw him too and moistened his lips.

'You want Garrett and Stanson, right?' he appealed to Thane quickly. 'We left them at the lodge, because they've got their own plans.' He gave a forced grin.

'Look, I'm tryin' to help. So watch that Stanson – he's a total headcase.'

Thane didn't answer but went over to Felix.

'I'm leaving you here with these two,' he said quietly. 'Can you handle it?'

Felix nodded gloomily.

'Radio to Henderson or whoever is running the Aviemore end now and tell them the score.' Thane paused, eyeing Angus Russell, reluctant to take him yet uncertain about leaving him. He sighed. 'All right, I can still use a driver, but nothing more. Understand?'

The leathery face hardly altered but the small, stocky man nodded.

Five minutes later they set off towards the Cailleach hill and the lodge. They were aboard MacLean's Land Rover because Russell's had suffered steering damage in the ramming collision. But the front towing brackets had remained intact and despite their protests MacLean and Joan Harton were now anchored by their handcuffs to the stout metal eyes.

They were removed from the reckoning. As the borrowed Land Rover began lurching along the track Thane caught a glimpse of Joe Felix giving a wave with his good arm before he turned away to use the radio.

He concentrated on what lay ahead, vaguely aware of Dunbar and Sandra Craig talking behind him, under the flapping canvas hood. Beside him, Russell gripped the steering wheel firmly, letting his body sway with the Land Rover's jolting movement.

'You reckoned about another mile to the lodge?' he asked Russell.

Russell nodded, peering ahead. They had only one headlamp still working and the alignment had been twisted. But, even so, Thane saw the landscape was gradually hardening, taking clearer shape as the moonlight began to give way to grey pre-dawn. He made up his mind.

'I want you to stop before there's any chance of us being seen from the lodge,' he said above the noise of the labouring engine. 'Can you do that, for certain?'

'Yes.' Russell gave him a quick sideways glance of curiosity but didn't comment. Whatever thoughts he had, he was keeping to himself.

The Cailleach hill gradually grew nearer. Then, suddenly, Russell flicked the gear-change into neutral, and let the vehicle coast to a halt.

'Try from up there,' he suggested curtly, switching off the engine and pointing to a stiff rise of ground ahead.

Thane beckoned to the others. Getting out, they followed Russell to the top of the rise and found themselves looking down a long, comparatively gentle slope of barren, rocky ground. Where it ended and the harsher, rising mass of the Cailleach hill began the grey pre-dawn let them see a small house. It was about a quarter mile away, and a thin chink of light showed from a window.

'They're still there.' The words came like a sigh from Russell. He gripped Thane's arm tightly. 'Well, what now?'

'You stay with the Land Rover – that was our bargain,' said Thane. He disengaged the man's hand from his arm, saw his expression, and gave a reassuring

190

nod. 'Don't worry, I've a job for you. I'm taking Francey with me and we're going down on foot. Give us twenty minutes to get into position, then I want the Land Rover to come driving down to the lodge as fast as you can bring it.'

Slow understanding dawned on Russell's face. Pushing back his beret, he scratched his bald head thoughtfully.

'There's a good chance they'll think it's MacLean coming back,' he said. 'And they'll want to know why.'

'I'm banking on it,' said Thane. 'Make as much noise as you want.'

'But what about me?' protested Sandra Craig.

'You'll be with Russell,' Thane told her. 'In reserve.'

'Why?' she asked indignantly.

Francey Dunbar chuckled without sympathy. 'Because he's the boss, love. Do what the nice super-intendent tells you.'

It took Thane and Dunbar ten of their twenty minutes to get down the slope. They stayed clear of the track and the result was a stumbling, cursing journey through a cold, downhill maze of broken rock and half-seen heather roots, each step a trap for the unwary.

A mountain hare exploded out from almost under their feet and streaked away. Startled, Francey Dunbar jumped sideways and splashed into an unsuspected saucer of soggy marsh. Cursing under his breath he got out of that and promptly tripped full length over a heather root.

191

'Stop clowning,' snarled Thane in a whisper, glancing back. 'Save it for your Federation meetings.'

Muttering obscenely, Dunbar struggled after him. At last, at the foot of the slope, they crouched down thankfully for a moment behind a clump of gorse and took their first close look at the shooting lodge. Situated about a hundred yards back from the track, it wasn't much bigger than the average cottage and had thick stone walls and a dark slate roof. A tiny front porch faced the track.

Other details took shape as they moved on, creeping from cover to cover in a cautious half-circle. The light they'd seen from the ridge came from a curtained front window and another chink of light showed at the window at the rear. There was a back door, and close by it the soft pulse of an electricity generator came from a small shed.

Then, as they eased back to their start point, Dunbar gave a sudden grunt of interest and pointed.

Thane had seen it too, the dark outline of a motor cycle propped against the wall beside the front porch. What looked like pannier bags were draped over the rear frame, behind the seat. The sight gave him a grim satisfaction. Stanson, at least, was still there and Stanson had come to matter to him almost as much as Garrett.

'Three minutes left,' murmured Dunbar, his thin face showing a trace of gathering tension. 'Sandra will be getting her knickers in a twist.'

Thane nodded, thinking of Angus Russell. Deliberately, he brought out the .38 Webley and checked it again.

'I'm on the front door, you take the back,' he said. 'If they catch on when the Land Rover comes down

192

and try the back way, take them. Either that or you'll hear me shout, and you get in that door, fast.'

'I won't knock,' promised Dunbar.

'Francey.' Thane stopped him as he went to wriggle away. 'Don't try to win any medals.'

'I've got one.' Dunbar grinned at him in the greyness. 'Poetry prize in my last year at school, but for God's sake don't tell anyone.'

He wriggled away.

Moments later Colin Thane made a crouching dash forward and flopped down behind his own final cover, a low mound of stones and rubble that appeared to be some previous owner's attempt at clearing ground for a garden patch. It was about twenty yards to the right of the front porch, the home of a few thistles and weeds and a symbol of someone's long-ago optimism.

He grimaced at the irrelevancy, shifted into a slightly more comfortable position, then tried to ignore the dry-mouthed tension building inside him while the seconds crawled past.

Then, suddenly, the rasp of the Land Rover's engine reached his ears and it appeared over the rise. A dark, lurching blob at first, the single headlamp beam stabbing down the slope like a wavering, drunken lance, it was travelling faster and more recklessly than he'd expected.

The crack of light at the lodge window widened as a curtain twitched. As if on cue, the Land Rover's horn sounded two raucous, urgent blasts, and the curtain fell closed again.

The porch door flew open, and more light poured out. A man was framed in it, another figure close behind him. Pete Stanson stepped out beyond the porch, staring at the approaching vehicle, an automatic held ready at his side, uncertain and hesitating as the Land Rover's horn sounded again.

Thane heaved himself up from cover, the Webley ready in his right hand – and at the same instant Stanson turned, saw him, and shouted a warning to the figure still half-concealed in the doorway. The gun in Stanson's hand swept up and barked viciously, the first shot wild, the second ricocheting off the stones beside Thane like an angry wasp.

Gripping the Webley two-handed, Thane felt it buck as he fired back, then had to throw himself down into cover as another gun slammed at him from the cottage doorway. Cursing, he triggered a shot in that direction, winced as another bullet from Stanson smashed into the rubble close to his head, rolled over to a new position, and saw Stanson running towards the parked motor cycle.

Thane fired again, missed his target, but heard the .38 calibre bullet smash into metal and an instant later a gush of fuel came from the motor cycle's ruptured fuel tank.

There was a fresh movement in the doorway. A shot slammed into the rubble close enough to spatter dirt into his face. Rolling frantically again, Thane triggered the Webley twice, saw the shape in the doorway lurch back, and heard a high-pitched roar as the motor cycle started up.

He half-rose, bringing the Webley up again as the trail bike snarled away with Stanson flattened low over the handlebars and fuel still spouting from the ruptured tank. In the background Thane heard a muffled crash coming from inside the cottage and someone shouting. But his attention was on Stanson – and, suddenly, as he trained the automatic on the fleeing rider, the Land Rover was there too.

Almost level with the lodge, it left the track in a wild, skidding turn and headed under full power in a jolting, pitching collision course at the motor cycle.

Stanson saw it coming. The trail bike's front wheel swung desperately, the rear tyre smoking rubber as it fought for grip.

It was too late. The Land Rover slammed its target, carrying man and machine grating beneath the front wheels for a few terrible moments before riding over them. As they were thrown aside there came a flat blast and a mushroom of fire. The ruptured fuel tank had exploded. Trapped under the twisted remains of the motor cycle, Stanson jerked and screamed for an instant while he burned like some obscene torch. Then he lay motionless, the flames still eating at his clothing, while the Land Rover came to a juddering halt some forty yards away.

A footstep on the porch brought him swinging round, still shaken but the Webley ready. Then he lowered it to his side, feeling weak, meeting Francey Dunbar's horrified eyes.

'Garrett?' asked Thane hoarsely.

'Inside.' Dunbar licked his lips. 'He'll keep.'

They ran towards the motor cycle and reached it just ahead of Russell and Sandra Craig, who had emerged from the Land Rover. They dragged Stanson clear, beat out the last few flames on his charred clothing with their bare hands, then Thane stopped, shook his head, and waved them back.

Stanson was dead. As Thane rose, Sandra Craig gave a sound like a whimper, then turned away and walked unsteadily back to the Land Rover.

She returned with an old coat. Angus Russell took it from her, and placed it over the dead man's head and shoulders. In the gathering dawn, his lined face showed a tired gravity which held neither triumph nor satisfaction.

'We'll be out here,' he said softly and, putting a hand on the girl's arm, led her away.

For a few seconds Thane stood where he was. A bird had begun singing somewhere on the hill, the sound incongruously sweet and clear above the low murmur of the wind and an occasional crackle from the cooling remains of the motor cycle.

'Sir, I –' Chewing an edge of his straggling moustache, shuffling his feet awkwardly, Francey Dunbar brought him back to the present. 'Hell, I kind of let you down. That damned back door held me up.'

'Forget it. I knew you were there.' Thane managed a lopsided, reassuring grin, then looked across at the lodge. 'What about Garrett?'

'I don't think he'll last long.' Dunbar shook his head soberly, answering Thane's unspoken question. 'He stopped a bullet in the chest – I just found him lying there when I got in.'

Together, they returned to the shooting lodge and as they went in from the little porch Thane could immediately smell the rank, sour odour of amphetamine. Through an open doorway off the tiny hall he saw a room laid out like a small laboratory, from glassware and gas cylinders to benches and chemical drums. But Dunbar nodded towards another doorway. Robin Garrett lay there, his shoulders resting against a bulky canvas rucksack.

'I took his gun,' said Dunbar. 'Just in case –'

Thane nodded. 'Look around.'

196

He bent over the man as Garrett's head turned on the rucksack pillow. His face was pale and strained, blood stained the front of his heavy sweater, and Thane silently noted the thick serge slacks he was wearing, the legs tucked into ankle-length climbing boots.

'Mopping up?' asked Garrett in a hoarse, unemotional voice. He watched Dunbar leave, then eyed Thane again. 'What happened to Stanson?'

'He didn't make it,' said Thane. 'We've got MacLean and Joan Harton.'

Garrett grimaced and gave a stifled cough. Red flecks of blood appeared on his lips and he licked them away with an effort.

'You holed a lung,' he said in the same hoarse, calm voice, and shrugged. 'Suits me – I've always been scared of rotting in a cell.' His eyes brightened. 'But we nearly made it – very nearly.' He coughed again, then asked, 'You know why I tried?'

Thane nodded. 'Your wife.'

'No.' Garrett shook his head. 'Both of us – equal shares. We were like two pieces of damned sandpaper, rubbing hell out of each other.' He licked his lips again. 'So I got the idea. Amphetamine's simple enough to make –'

'I was told,' said Thane quietly.

'The Copenhagen syndicate would have gone to a million pounds sterling – a million.' Garrett forced himself up a fraction, grinned hideously, then sank back with another choking cough. 'Then Pender got himself killed – and afterwards that damned little maniac Stanson panicked and tried to run you down. That started you, right?'

197

Thane shook his head. 'Earlier, though it was mostly guesswork. How did you get your team together?'

'The amateur way – asked them.' Garrett's voice faded, then rose again. 'MacLean first, when I caught him thieving in the distillery. I knew young Russell's background and he brought in Stanson – they both wanted money.'

'And Joan Harton?'

'Joan?' A slight cynical smile touched the man's lips. 'I found her in London. She had contacts – and she's got other assets.' He grimaced. 'But then when we were almost through it all started going sour.'

'Including Benodet.' Thane found his handkerchief and wiped the dying man's lips. 'Don't you want to know about Sean Russell?'

'He's dead, I suppose.' Garrett closed his eyes for a moment as Thane nodded. 'If that basket Benodet hadn't tried to move in, if – if he hadn't traced us after Stanson killed his man in Glasgow –' The coughing came again, an uncontrollable spasm, and when he stopped his breathing came quick and shallow, a rasping, bubbling sound.

Francey Dunbar had returned. He hesitated, then backed away as Thane shook his head.

'Thanks,' said Garrett in a whisper, 'I don't feel like an audience.' He grimaced. 'You came half an hour too soon.'

'You'd have been gone?'

Garrett nodded. 'See this rucksack? Half our last production run is stowed in it – the moment the light was good enough I'd have been back-packing it out on foot, not to Aviemore but the other way. Clean over the hills.' He stared defiantly at Thane, 'I – hell, I could have made it.'

198

'Maybe.' Thane could believe him, though it was a long, punishing trek, and only a man who knew his mountains could have made it. 'To where?'

'Braemar.' Garrett struggled for breath, and forced a grin. 'Would you have thought of that?'

'Somebody might.' Thane bent closer to the man, sensing time was running out. 'Where's the rest of it – the earlier runs?'

'Same place – Braemar. Woman in a boarding house there keeps a – a trunk for me. Thinks I'm a mad climber who likes a change of clothes.' The rasping, bubbling breathing grew louder for an instant, then Garrett tried twice to shape his words before they came. 'I'd try it again. For a million – and to be my own man. What do you say to that, Thane?'

'Ever seen a junkie?' asked Thane quietly.

He waited for an answer. It didn't come. Garrett's eyes had closed. His head lolled on the rucksack and then the bubbling noise stopped.

An hour later a convoy of Northern Constabulary vehicles crawled down the track and reached the lodge. They had Joe Felix with them, and the two prisoners.

Sergeant Henderson and a lanky, worried-looking local detective inspector talked with Thane briefly. Then, as the detective inspector left, his main thoughts obviously on the nightmare of reports and paperwork ahead, Henderson hung back.

'Aye, it's been rough.' The elderly sergeant produced his cigarettes, gave one to Thane, took one himself, and they shared a light. Then, as Thane drew on the smoke, he added quietly, 'We got the bodies out of Benodet's car.'

'And?' Something in Henderson's manner made Thane raise a questioning eyebrow.

'We had a doctor along by then,' said Henderson slowly. 'Sean Russell didn't drown. In fact, it looks like he was dead in that luggage boot long before the car went over.'

'Is he sure?' Thane stared at him.

Henderson shrugged. 'He says not till the full autopsy report, but I know our man and he doesn't take chances. Russell had been clubbed on the head and had a fractured skull. The odds are he didn't live an hour after Benodet grabbed him. After that, Benodet must have been bluffing his way along.' He paused, smiled slightly, and added, 'I thought you'd want to know.'

'Yes.' Thane drew a deep breath with the feeling he'd been freed from the major part of a personal nightmare. 'Thanks.'

He walked out of the lodge into the morning. It should have been bright sunlight, but it was raining hard and a biting wind had sprung up.

He didn't care.

It was two days later, about mid-morning, before the time came when Thane could leave Aviemore. By then, a lot had happened, much of it routine, all of it necessary.

Margaret Garrett had come back from Edinburgh and had listened to the story white-faced, then had walked away not quite dry-eyed. Charged and cautioned, facing the inevitable and talking freely, Joan Harton and Shug MacLean had begun the long wait for their day in court. The rest of the amphetamine had been recovered from the Braemar boarding house. Several packing cases filled with future court productions had been removed from the shooting lodge.

The rest had been a small mountain of written statements, the delicate diplomacy of handing the case over to the Northern Constabulary's jurisdiction, the telephone calls which had passed to and from the Scottish Crime Squad headquarters in Glasgow.

Between times, Thane had managed to telephone home twice. Then finally, by arrangement, he made another phone call just before he left. It was to the Western Infirmary.

'Wrapped it up?' asked Phil Moss when he came on the line in his hospital ward.

'All that matters.' Thane kept his manner casual. 'How about you?'

'No complaints,' answered Moss almost as casually. 'You – uh – heard about the payroll business?'

'I heard,' said Thane.

He grinned at the receiver. From Moss's hunch onward about his fellow patient it had all fitted together. Charlie Grunion, suddenly deprived of his inside man, had been an anxious visitor, then had still made his try for the payroll truck. On the Friday it had gone out on its usual route and timings, and Grunion, with two car-loads of neds, had ambushed it in a dockside street in Millside Division. Twelve of the largest cops in the Division had poured out of the truck and had gathered them up.

'One other thing,' said Moss cautiously. 'Buddha Ilford came visiting. I've got a new job when I get out of here, at Headquarters.'

'What kind?' Thane wondered what was coming.

'He wants a liaison officer. Someone to poke around, find out what's going on and keep him in

201

touch,' said Moss and gave a dry grunt. 'I – uh – I can give it a try.'

'I'll give you a tip,' said Thane seriously. 'Buddha likes his coffee weak – and two lumps of sugar.'

'Go to hell,' said Moss indignantly, and hung up.

Grinning, Thane left the police station. It was a warm, bright day outside, he'd already said goodbye to Henderson, and the two Scottish Crime Squad cars were lined up waiting. Francey Dunbar lounged against the Ford. Still with his arm in a sling, Joe Felix was talking to Sandra Craig.

'Time to go home,' said Thane as he reached them. Then he frowned. 'No, one thing first – priority.'

'Sir?' Francey Dunbar blinked. 'We've done everything, even down to our overtime sheets.' He appealed to the others. 'Right?'

They nodded.

'If we're going to be a team, there are two things you sure are going to have to remember,' said Thane heavily. 'First, don't mention overtime – that stops when anyone is fool enough to be promoted from chief inspector. The other thing –' he paused and grinned – 'the other thing is to get your priorities right. We've got to find a trout farm.'

'A what?' Dunbar goggled at him.

'A trout farm,' repeated Thane patiently. 'My wife wants some, Maggie Fyffe wants some. Understand?'

'Trout,' sighed Dunbar.

'They're fish,' agreed Felix.

'Can we get them ready-cooked?' asked Sandra Craig. She gestured unhappily. 'Well, why not? I'm hungry.'

They got into the cars and set off.

21